THE LEGEND AND THE MAN

When Morgan headed south across the Rio Grande on an impossible mission, he wasn't alone. No gunfighter turned down the chance to venture into Old Mexico with a legend like Morgan. Ten of them reached the besieged Spanish fortress of Hacienda St Leque, but even before fighting their way in, men were dying at the hands of Colonel Moro and his sombreroed butchers. Many more would fall before Morgan rode out alone to kill the colonel — or die trying . . .

Books by Ben Nicholas
in the Linford Western Library:

THIS MAN KILLS
BLOOD KIN
BADLANDERS

BEN NICHOLAS

THE LEGEND AND THE MAN

Complete and Unabridged

LINFORD
Leicester

First published in Great Britain in 2006 by
Robert Hale Limited
London

First Linford Edition
published 2007
by arrangement with
Robert Hale Limited
London

British Library CIP Data

Nicholas, Ben
   The legend and the man.—Large print
ed.—Linford western library
1. Western stories
2. Large type books
I. Title
823.9'2 [F]

ISBN 978–1–84782–016–7

Published by
F. A. Thorpe (Publishing)
Anstey, Leicestershire

Set by Words & Graphics Ltd.
Anstey, Leicestershire
Printed and bound in Great Britain by
T. J. International Ltd., Padstow, Cornwall

This book is printed on acid-free paper

1

MISSION TO MEXICO

Gloom came prematurely to the warped and twisted streets of Waco Flats that day as a heavy cover of cloud rolled in from over the sullen gray hills.

Chimney-pots smoked and lamps began to burn in saloons, liveries, the apothecary's, the blackmith's and the Zia cantina. All else appeared clothed in gloom, the alleys running off the twisted main street already dark and mysterious.

Two tall men, one lean and well-made, his companion heavy and slouched, appeared silently on the stoop of the unlit wagon shop directly across the street from the cantina. They had come from the alley leading to the closest livery — where they'd inspected every horse carefully before making their silent way to what was jokingly known as the main street.

The pair stood motionless for a time in the shadows, staring bleakly across at the saloon, its early light reflected dimly in their eyes. The eyes of the larger, older man were chocolate-brown, his youthful companion's a singular chill shade of gray.

'That's his hoss,' the first man grunted, nodding towards the roman-nosed black with a heavy Spanish-Texas saddle strapped to its broad back. A bedroll encased in a yellow groundsheet was lashed behind the saddle and the stock of a rifle thrust up from the saddle scabbard. 'Only someone like him would have the brass to leave good gear like that around for any light-finger to hitch.'

The man's voice was deep and rough-edged, yet the clear ear of his companion detected a flaw in its timbre. He was afraid.

The younger man took a match from between his teeth. He was around

twenty-five, his face strikingly handsome in a chiseled, high-cheekboned
way. In the half-gloom the well-spaced
eyes appeared normal but in bright
light could take on the empty, icy look
of chips of spun glass.

'Let's get it done,' he grunted and
stepped down into the rutted street. He
had a jauntiness, a self-confident grace
that commanded attention.

He covered several paces before
realizing he was alone. He propped and
whirled, his eyes seeming to glow in the
dark like an animal's.

'What?' His voice was cold as
knife-steel.

'I . . . I'm sorry, Flash . . . but I jest
cain't do it.' He spread trembling
hands, a hard man turned to jelly. 'It
was bad enough seein' all them others'
pards at the livery . . . but when you
add Morgan to the mix . . . I . . . '

'Like they say, scum will always rise
to the surface if you give it time!'

The younger man's voice dripped
with venom and contempt. But there

was control as well. At another time he might well have whipped out a gun and shot his henchman where he stood; it would be anything but the first. But his gun remained in its holster and now he was turning his back and continuing across the thoroughfare alone, jaws locked with steely self-control. He could not allow himself to be distracted at this late stage, not after coming so far.

Eschewing the steps he sprang directly from ground to saloon porch and landed like a heavy-muscled cat. The music spilling out over the batwings was a discordant mix of guitar, piano and a strident contralto. But the newcomer was hearing only sonorous strains of Beethoven in the cage of his skull as he shouldered through the swinging doors, sighted his man immediately and filled his lungs to shout.

'Morgan!'

The shout cutting through the border saloon like a gunshot simply shouted danger, and when they focused on a silhouette, tall, well-built and plainly enraged standing just beyond the reach of a slowly fading overhead swinging light, drunks, cowboys, painted women and ashen-faced towners hustled wildly away from him as if someone had just yelled 'Plague!'

It was reckless to barge into any bordertown dive in such a brazen manner — doubly so when the place in question happened to be playing host to a bunch of Arizonan mercenaries heading south into Old Mexico that night.

A man could get himself killed, pulling that sort of fool caper. Hands had grabbed gun-handles and trigger-fingers were at the ready as some of the fastest guns in the country watched and waited for the newcomer to move into full light.

Standing at the back bar, his face dark and expressionless, Morgan didn't move a muscle. He didn't need good light or an introduction to know exactly who it was who'd called his name.

He asked himself with a sigh: How often had some hired gun, some killer with a grudge or merely some empty-headed gunkid looking to score some points announced himself in just such a way as this?

There were times when a gun professional like Morgan felt he couldn't get enough sixgun action. Yet every so often a man felt his soul grow weary of the blood and danger, the violent monotony of his chosen style of living.

With dead men in back of him and the likelihood of big killing ahead, Morgan was sunk in one of those low moods tonight. Last thing he was looking for at the Zia cantina was trouble, gun trouble least of all.

He stared bleakly as a tall and wide-shouldered figure, as graceful and lithe as a blood thoroughbred, moved directly beneath a big fuming oil-lamp, and greasy yellow light spilled over familiar features.

Damaron!

Morgan continued to remain both motionless and expressionless as he watched one of the deadliest gunfighters he'd ever seen move to the bar and slap down on it hard with the flat of his hand.

'Water! And I'll take it straight!'

That was Damaron, the big man brooded. The man was simply different. He rode a slow horse, favored ugly women, professed to be a devotee of the Lord — and drank water rather than bourbon, tequila, even coffee.

Some claimed the gunman affected these idiosyncrasies merely to attract attention. Morgan knew better. Flash Damaron acted different because that was how he was. Different and very dangerous, even judged by the standards of one of the top guntippers in the Southwest. Himself.

Damaron had started out not very different from the rest of the breed — a vicious gun-punk ready to do anything for cash or thrills. Mostly that breed ended up dead or doing a life hitch in

Yuma before they reached twenty. Not Damaron. He was different. A combination of dumb luck, bravado and dazzling gunskills had seen the former gunkid mature into the genuine article — a gun master.

Morgan knew exactly just how dangerous this gunman with the looks and style of a Broadway actor really was. He also knew him to be an A-grade son of a bitch.

It was cold comfort to know that almost everyone who knew Flash Damaron well hated him. This despite the fact that he was a man with a desperate need to be liked, admired, respected for what he was. But, of course, hand in hand with any man's hatred for the gunfighter, walked fear. Any man had to be at least a little scared of this one whom the dusk had brought to Waco Flats. Either that or he was a fool. One or the other.

Which was the reason deadly hands slid off gun handles, and none saw fit to block the gunslinger's path as, his gaze finally settling upon big Morgan, the newcomer threaded his lithe-footed way between the crowded tables towards him.

Only Buck Clooney, loyal, dependable Buck from the early days, showed ready and willing to stand by him and make a play should Morgan see fit.

'Looks ornery, Morg,' the Kentuckian said from the corner of his mouth. 'Mebbe I should cut the bastard down while we got an edge — '

'No!' Morgan was emphatic. He had a strong feeling that the gunslinger had not come here looking to raise any kind of gun hell. Instead he sensed it was vanity that had brought Damaron to the borderlands. Wounded vanity.

He was right.

'So, big man,' Damaron strode up to the back bar and stood with hands on hips, handsome features virtually blank but for the eyes, 'you finally got to be so big that you figgered you could do without loyal old pards, huh?'

So that was it, Morgan thought. The

man's nose was out of joint. When Morgan had gone about scouring the jailhouses, low dives, outlaw hideouts and feral lairs to muster his special mercenary force this time, he'd avoided Temple Gulch, home base of some of the finest guntippers in the bloody trade — including the man standing before him.

The newcomer was right about his being overlooked for the big one, but dead wrong in referring to himself as an 'old pard.' They'd never been that; not the formidable 'Morg' Morgan and lightning-bolt Damaron. They had worked together once or twice but it took more than that to make men pards. And following the Spanish Bit assignment Morgan had vowed never to work with this gun again.

Sure, this high-stepper was good. They didn't come better with knives, guns or just standing cool and tough against the odds. But Morgan simply didn't take to him. The fast gun was too filled with arrogance and brag, too swift to take offence and far too ready with a .45. To round out his persona, Flash Damaron was also much given to envy and jealousy.

But the man's prime failing was his ambition. It was not enough for him to be recognized as what he was — a genuine gun prince. He wanted the lot — status, respect, loyalty — even love.

And he'd never get all those baubles. Not even from the everyday artisans of the sixgun brotherhood, much less from the top-notchers, the ones who really counted.

Clay Morgan was a gunfighter, just like Damaron, yet they were vastly different in almost every way that counted. The big man was a loner by nature yet somehow or other always found himself working with gangs, such as this one he'd put together over the past ten days in Arizona. Even men who didn't like him would follow him anyplace. Yet he never did anything conscious or overt to win that respect and this riled Damaron worse than anything.

Morgan never tried to charm anybody. Folks were free to like him or hate him — it never meant a crosswise damn to him either way.

All he wanted out of life was to stay alive as long as he could and die with his boots on. Some claimed Morgan would live forever. On the other hand there were always stories circulating that Damaron had finally stopped the death bullet he'd been begging for all his life. It was as though his enemies reckoned that if they hatched up enough death stories like that, one might come true some day, and the sooner the better.

Morgan never believed such stories, not even when the odd one made it into the obituaries in the newspapers. He believed Damaron would prove as hard to kill as any man he'd ever known. But he also knew no man of the gun lived for ever.

He said, 'What are you drinking, Flash?'

Damaron swiped a beer-bottle off the bar. His eyes glittered brightly.

'Don't hand me that palavery bullshit, big man! I never trailed you all the way from Paiute County to drink with you. I'm here to find out why you handed me the biggest goddamn insult of my life!'

The saloon stirred uneasily. Men muttered nervously behind muffling hands as a mournful wind moaned outside, tempting a broken slat loose.

A mean streak was riding Damaron hard, that much was plain even if Morgan's bunch weren't sure what was behind it. Only the mercenary leader had understood what was going on from the moment the guntipper first appeared.

'You weren't on my list, Flash. Simple as that.'

Damaron's face turned pale. 'You are sayin' I ain't good enough to ride with you against a scumsucker like Colonel goddamn Moro?'

Instantly Morgan realized that the

gunfighter had inside knowledge of the expedition. The deal down at Hacienda St Leque was intended to be secret but the man standing before him had winkled it out somehow. He was the type who'd smash information out of a man who would not supply it voluntarily.

'Maybe next time?' he said, snapping his fingers at the bartender. 'Now . . . water with something, maybe?'

'Go straight to hell, big man! We both of us know I'm a better fighting man than any of these stumble-bum losers you've rounded up.' He paused, then had to add. 'I'm better than you, if it comes to that!'

A sucked-out silence filled the room for a moment, followed by a rushed flurry of scraping feet as nervous drinkers moved away in fear of gunplay.

But some of the panic subsided as Morgan folded his arms across his chest and spoke in a measured voice:

'You could be right, mister. But we'll never know, will we?'

'Yeller!' the gunslinger flared. Then he whirled to face the gunfighters, waving his arms. 'Yeller and a con — that's the sort of geezer you're willin' to follow. What? You mean to say you didn't know this St Leque thing is a big sham? You poor dumb bastards — Morgan never signed on for this job for money or glory or on account he got bored playin' gun-god to the morons in Flagstaff and Dallas.'

He wheeled and wagged an angry finger in Morgan's face.

'Tell 'em it's the woman, big man. And don't say it ain't. Don Julius's wife down at St Leque, to be perzack. That crazy, good-lookin' one what you got all tangled up with up before when — '

'Shut your mouth, Damaron!' It was Buck Clooney who cut in. Clooney knew Morgan better than anyone and realized this was plainly something the big man didn't want spread about right now. In particular that reference to the Don's wife being 'loco'.

He moved to place himself squarely

between the gunfighter and the scowling Morgan, and jabbed Damaron in the chest. 'Pack your traps and dust afore you open that big mouth of yours wide enough for you to dig your own lousy grave with it!'

'I'm talkin' to the butcher and not the block, Clooney,' snarled Damaron, slapping the hand away. 'And what I'm tellin' you is nothin' but the simple goddamn truth.'

His sweeping gesture encompassed the entire room.

'I've got the right to let you bunch of second-raters know just what it is you're lettin' yourselves in for down south. I know Morgan sold you tenth-raters a big line about helpin' out good folks in trouble and gettin' to take a cut at that son-of-a-whore, Moro. But you oughta know that if Don Julius wasn't wed to a woman he lusts after, and if that woman wasn't in mighty deep danger right now as I speak, along with the rest of those stinkin' rich geezers down there, then there'd be no ridin' to St Leque, no promise of big money and action aplenty. Nothin'!'

'One more word!' warned Clooney.

'This is two, but they come from the heart, tenth-rater. Turn green!'

With the words, Damaron let fly with a driving right that crashed into Clooney's jaw, sending the big man flying. As Clooney crashed to the floor, Damaron's momentum carried him into Morgan's range.

A big fist travelled less than a foot to explode against the gunslinger's jaw. Flash Damaron went down like a cold beer in a Rio Grande heatwave.

As the unconscious figure slammed into the floor and rolled twice, Morgan's voice carried to every corner of the saloon.

'If we were to hang around here until this man comes to I'd have to kill him, and I don't have the time or the stomach for that.' He flipped his hat and caught it. 'So we're leaving now and will be in Mexico in an hour. Any of you boys who heard what he said and don't like the sound of the job can drop out right here and now, if he wants. No pay, but no hard feelings neither. For everybody else, haul your freight right now. We're leaving!'

He strode for the batwings and men followed him out. Shortly the muffled drumbeat of hoofs was to be heard, carrying the Morgan gang southward for the border.

The complete gang.

Morgan never voiced a word of thanks for their loyalty. Nor did he venture to throw any light on Damaron's allegations. All he did in fact was to post men at various points along their backtrail, with orders to take the gunslinger out should he attempt to follow them across the border. You could not be too careful with a hellion of that caliber.

But there was no sign of the gunslinger that night, nor the next. When the band reached the foothills of the Toro Sierras several days later, they heard the news that Damaron had attempted to blast his way through a border checkpoint and had drawn a ten-year stretch on the rock pile in some stinking Mexican prison for his pains. But he escaped a short while later.

How Morgan felt about this turn of events wasn't known as he didn't comment. He was too busy gathering fresh information concerning the siege of Hacienda St Leque.

What he heard suggested the situation in Valley Moritomo might not be as bad as he had expected.

It sounded worse.

* * *

The fortress that was Hacienda St Leque stood as mighty and imposing as it had always done despite the fact that its power, and the power of the don, had been greatly diminished in recent times. The Diaz family had ruled this section of Valley Moritomo for three generations. Their authority had never been seriously challenged before. Now, after almost a hundred years, it appeared that the lush valley might be lost to them for good.

Months earlier the valley peasants had risen against Don Julius Diaz, accusing him of being a 'decadent immoral aristocrat.' The rebellion might have simply petered out in time if it hadn't been for intervention of the army. The soldiers led by the notorious Colonel Moro had been able to crush the peasants' revolt, while at the same time taking advantage of the situation to turn on Diaz 'in the name of the people,' which led to the eventual confinement of the family and its army of friends, relatives and supporters to the great natural fortress of the hilltop hacienda itself.

The resulting siege, long, bloody and costly, had not been foreseen by the treacherous Colonel. When Moro first hatched his notion of supporting the rebellious peons in order to overthrow the don, his real criminal intention had been to take possession of the great hacienda himself, one of the proudest most luxurious palaces-cum-fortresses in the entire province.

But the original Don Julius had built his handsome hilltop fortress hacienda, with its lovely garden courts and the netherworld of cellars and tunnels, to withstand any foe. So it was that when successor Don Julius Diaz withdrew to his fortress and raised the drawbridge over the moat, the tall stone walls and the courage of the defenders proved too defiant and strong for the enemy at the gates.

Now the peons who believed they'd regain their freedom from oppression once the Don was overthrown, were discovering what real repression could be like. The moment he had the *ricos* trapped in the great hacienda Colonel Moro had quickly dropped his pretext of 'liberator of the poor.' He promptly confiscated the peons' arms and had the valley elders executed. So the entire valley came under the iron heel of the military.

Of course it was not legal.

Yet whatever else the colonel did in Moritomo, he managed to keep what had once been a troublesome province reasonably peaceful and rebel-free. Mexico City chose to turn a blind eye upon what was taking place in the valley. Even though it knew that some one hundred aristocratic Mexicans and their retinues were existing in a state of permanent siege at 'Fortress' St Leque, it did nothing to assist them in their plight.

During the initial months of the siege Don Julius had lived well, to the point of luxury. The don was a very wealthy man. His cellars were lavishly stocked with fine wine and provisions. His 'court' as he called it, was cultivated and attractive, his retainers loyal. But most important of all to a man of his arrogance and vanity, he was still lord and master here if noplace else.

But in time the restrictions began to take their toll and the don cast about for a way to bring an increasingly intolerable situation to an end.

Standing upon his parapets he would gaze out over the verdant valley that he had once ruled, toward the Torro Sierras where he'd once hunted with falcon and rifle and which were now peopled with alien troopers in gray tunics and black hats — and ponder how he might change it all back to the way it had been.

The solution never dawned, or at least not upon Don Julius. It was his handsome wife, Doña Iselda, who eventually came up with the plan.

Doña Iselda knew a certain *Americano* named Morgan, a notorious mercenary. How she knew him she chose not to reveal, and the don did not ask. She believed she could exert some influence upon this man, she told her husband. If he were to make contact with this Morgan and beg him to raise a force and attempt to free them from the siege . . . ? It was a slender hope, she had insisted, yet it was surely all they had.

Reluctantly, Don Julius agreed. Doña Iselda drafted the request for her husband to send to Pueblo County, Arizona Territory. The communication read more like a command than a plea for help but in time it drew a reply from Morgan, informing them that he was on his way. Just as Doña Iselda had expected.

And so the don spent much of his spare time gazing out over the valley from his encircled fortress searching for the first sign of his wife's gringo friend.

Yet the don was plagued by grave doubts.

The siege had lasted for five months now and supplies were running low. Yet the doña remained stubbornly sure of her man.

'He will come, my husband,' she insisted, joining him on the parapets late that afternoon. 'He said he would, therefore he shall. *Por favor*, just be patient.'

The don, small, erect and stiff-backed, cocked an eyebrow and studied his lady.

The marriage between the arrogant, impetuous Don Julius and his dark Iselda had been a success. She was sometimes eccentric, it was true. Some even suggested she was much more than that. But it was only her spirit and her passion that made her seem that way to others, so her husband believed. He had learned to put up with her peculiar ways, her obsessiveness towards their daughter, Lucetta, even her own infidelities.

Tall and raven-tressed, Iselda appeared lovelier at forty than she had done on their wedding-day; the don was justly proud of her.

It was only natural that a woman of her beauty and charm should attract admirers. And the don must admit that her power over men had proved highly useful in the past. Don Julius had freely exploited his wife's talents for seduction in order to advance his own ambitions over the years, and possessed a highly un-Spanish tolerance for marital infidelity. He himself boasted a string of mistresses ranging from high-born aristocrats to low-life strumpets, so why should not his doña also enjoy the occasional discreet liaison?

He was confident that the relationship with the gringo, Morgan, was nothing more than a diversion for Doña Iselda. How could it be otherwise? She had bedded princes and American millionaires before and had never been tempted to abandon him and their opulent life in the valley. How could some rough-hewn American *pistolero* succeed where so many others had failed?

But naturally Morgan was smitten. Iselda had told him so one uneasy night, following a major enemy assault upon Hacienda St Leque.

'This *hombre* is like no other, my husband,' she had told him. Her eyes glowed as she spoke and the don had found himself vaguely irritated. 'He is a brute — huge, fearless and greatly respected. If any man could save us from Moro, then this man can.'

'One man against hundreds?'

'Morgan rarely works alone. He has made a reputation upon his proven ability to recruit other mercenaries like himself and put them in the field quickly, when required. His hand-picked followers are fast, ruthless and totally loyal to their leader. With a band of just ten men he has succeeded at things not even an army could accomplish. I swear he is our best hope, Julius.'

'But would he come, Iselda?'

'He will come.'

And such had proved to be the case. They had made contact, Morgan had replied in the affirmative, hopes soared.

But that was ten days ago now, so the don reminded himself with a pensive frown as he lighted a fragrant cigarillo and drew deeply. True, it was a long and risky journey from Arizona to the valley, but surely the man should have

27

been here by this?

And imagining all the disasters that might have befallen the Morgan party, he felt a cold dread stirring in his bowels.

The gringo mercenary was their only hope now. If he did not come . . .

Diaz could see them, right at that low moment of his long day. Down there in the valley over which he had once ruled with such a magnificent totality of authority — Moro's gray-garbed troopers in their dugouts and hide-holes, the caves and the trenches with which they had formed a complete ring encircling them. The accursed colonel had long since surrendered his campaign to take the hacienda by force — it had proved far too strong to penetrate. Starvation was proving a longer but more certain plan of conquest.

Such was Diaz's notoriety as an anti-government, peon-hating martinet that in his hour of peril he found himself with nobody to call upon for help. Nobody, that was, but a gringo gunman who had slept with his wife!

The don's mood was plummeting by the minute and it hardly helped any when, from out of the blue, Doña Iselda said, in that strange, abstracted way of hers, 'Of course he shall come . . . if only to save the princess . . . '

He stared at her. Of course, the don loved his daughter, but not in the same way as did his wife. On the very day of Lucetta's birth, nineteen years earlier, Diaz became aware that he had been instantly relegated to second place in his wife's affection. Lucetta became overnight the centerpiece of the doña's entire life, and the very fact that at times the don considered his daughter to be cold, distant and even downright disloyal, never seemed in any way to impinge on his wife's devotion towards the girl.

So it was typical that, in this uncertain hour, Doña Iselda should be thinking not of her own safety or her husband's, or that of the hundreds of others imprisoned with them up here but rather that of just one person — Lucetta.

Perhaps it might be true what the medico from Taos had confided to Diaz last year when he attended the doña for pneumonia. The man suggested that the mother's eccentricity was developing into something more sinister. Her moments of abstraction appeared to be occurring with increasing frequency. Naturally Don Julius shied away from the word 'insanity' but sometimes felt that the woman he had once loved so deeply had become a stranger. Raising his eyes heavenwards Don Julius silently demanded to know just what he had done to deserve such burdens.

Again it was his wife who diverted him. 'Look!' she cried, shuddering as she pointed toward the blue sierras. 'Devil birds!'

Don Julius gazed westwards to see the buzzards circling above a shadowy canyon. The scavengers, once rare in the valley, had become commonplace since Moro had overrun the valley and the siege and the cruelty had begun.

A deep melancholy stole over the aristo as he watched the macabre, creatures gliding in over the lonely mountainsides. It was hard for him to believe that just a few short months previously he had ruled this land like a colossus, master of all he surveyed. Now he lived like a caged beast, still snarling defiance at his tormentors but growing weaker and less assured with every passing day, staking all his hopes upon some gringo adventurer he didn't even know.

For one hundred years his family had ruled here, now it would end like this — his own countrymen turning their backs when he most needed them and Moro circling below, waiting for the day when his defences would collapse and they would come to feed on his bones.

It was Don Julius's lowest point ever. The irony of this was that in this very hour of doubt, despair and self-doubt, help was closer than it had been at any time since Colonel Moro marched into his valley.

2

LAND OF THE DON

Morgan puffed on a cheroot, watching Waldo walk back from inspecting the dead on the bloody hillside, angry, disturbed buzzards screeching overhead.

'Seven of 'em, Morg,' the young gun reported in his lazy drawl. 'Hogtied then shot in the back of the head. Peons, by the looks.'

Morgan exhaled a cloud of blue smoke and stared bleakly south, the direction they were heading. Mexico was a furnace that day. The heat added to the stink and the air of desolation which held this ugly mesa foothill in its grip.

'How is it,' Dundee asked rhetorically, 'that when anybody gets it in the neck down here in *mañana*-land, it's always the poor?'

'How is it,' countered Morgan, 'that we're running low on water and you're sitting your saddle running off at the mouth instead of scouting for a creek?'

You couldn't rattle Dundee. The Texan-born former cavalryman with Jeb Stuart just winked at the others and turned his dun away to attend to his chore. Chiller, Wyatt and Waldo watched him ride away before returning their attention to Morgan.

The deeper they struck into the province the more frequent were the signs of violence and murder, sure indicators that their ultimate destination was not shaping up as any kind of beer-and-hamper picnic. But then, none expected anything different.

The riders expected Morgan to give the signal to get under way, but had forgotten he'd also sent Kit Chiller to scout the vicinity while Waldo inspected the dead.

Morgan hunkered down on a dead-fall and took out his sixshooter. He pushed a scrap of rag through the barrel with the cleaning-rod. He repeated the process several times, and held the muzzle to his eye to peer down the mirror shine of the barrel. He tested the action and replaced the piece as a shadow fell across him. He looked up into lanky Buck Clooney's homely mug.

'What?' he growled. He knew that look. The Iowan was the closest thing he had to a partner in the whole bunch, although he'd eat dirt before he'd admit it.

'Damaron, that's what.'

'What about him?'

'What about him?' Clooney sounded testy. 'What do you mean, 'what about him?' You reckon he's just gonna shrug and forget about what happened across the Rio?'

Morgan looked away.

'He came looking for trouble and he found it. End of story.'

Clooney hunkered down on his spurs in front of him and stared him in the eye.

'You know, at times like this you can act like the dumbest dumb-ass that ever walked, Morg. We're talkin' Damaron, not Joe Nobody. That geezer came God alone knows how far to face you down about not huntin' him up for this job. He wanted to sound off some, then have you back-water and sign him on. Any whiskey-soak in that joint could have seen that. Instead you knock him on his ass and we'd have been half-way to the Rio by the time he was able to sit a saddle. And you reckon he'd take all that off of you in front of a whole damn town — him that reckons he's the best and the purtiest thing that ever was — and just do nothin'?'

'What's he gonna do, worry-wart? Come after me?' Morgan's gesture encompassed the scene surrounding them: ten gunfighters enjoying the noon break, mostly calmly eating, tending guns and horses, each man composed and lethal-looking in a way that would distinguish him in any company any-place. 'And them, for God's sake?'

Clooney looked uncertain.

'Well, I'm not sayin' he'd be that much of a dumb-ass. But, Judas, Morg, that flash bastard hates harder than anyone I know, and I reckon that at least we oughta — '

'Not be shying at shadows,' Morgan finished for him, getting to his feet. He frowned, then grinned. 'Look, if it'll make you feel better, I'll have Dundee ride drag and keep a look-out behind . . . just in case you're right and I'm wrong. How's that?'

Clooney grinned. 'All right, I guess. Hey, here comes Chiller now.'

The slim-hipped Kansan came loping back through the coarse grass and reined in before them.

'They was shot sometime yesterday by soldiers wearin' them flashy, high-heeled cavalrymen's boots they seem to favor down here, Morg. Back yonder, they scrawled a message in the dust in Spanish what read: 'Let this be a warning to the whole accursed valley. Support your ruler or die'.'

Morgan flicked his cigar butt on to a rocky patch. 'Moro, for sure,' he grunted. 'They all hold life cheap down here, but that bastard doesn't set a price on it at all.'

'So, Moro is the one we'll be goin' up against then, Morg?'

'Uh-huh. He's the one who decided to boot Don Julius out of his valley and now's got him holed up atop that big pile of stone we sighted with the glasses from back at Lucetta Point.'

He paused, squinting south. Then: 'Let's dust!'

'Action stations, *amigos*!' Young Ken Waldo grinned, expelling twin jets of cigarette smoke through his nostrils. 'Hands up who's sorry he left the old Rio Grande behind him, now you can smell the dead men? C'mon, be honest.'

There was no response but spirits were high as the riders crossed a low hillcrest and moved from the walk into the lope. They could smell action on the wind and most were either young enough or crazy enough to be excited by it.

The only sober face belonged to Buck Clooney. Clooney had been in Fort Jackson, Arizona, when Doña Iselda and her party visited a year earlier. He knew now that what Flash Damaron had said back across the border was true — Morgan was doing this for a woman.

He brought his cayuse alongside Morgan as they put the hill behind them and followed a winding trail down.

'How strong is this Moro geezer, Morg?'

'That's what we're about to find out.'

'Well, I was just actin' dumb. Y'see, I happen to know he's Commander, Army Post Nineteen, Los Lunas. If that's a regular post, like I guess it would be, then he's likely commandin' upwards of two hundred troopers.'

'So?'

'There's ten of us.'

'And?'

'Hell! Them sort of odds just ain't — '

'Don't give me that bullcrap, Buck. You've never fretted about odds before. Not once. Why don't you come straight out with it? You haven't been happy about this job from the get-go, and I know why. But I'm going to make you say it.'

Clooney showed no emotion. He was accustomed to the other's hard ways. They'd been together a long time. He liked to think they were partners, but with Morgan you could never be sure.

'All right,' he said, 'if that's how you want it. It's . . . it's unlucky, that's what it is.'

'What's unlucky?'

'Riskin' a passel of good men's lives over somethin' you got goin' with that woman. There, you made me say it and I hope you don't like it!'

'So,' Morgan said, slit-eyed and hard-jawed. 'Still sailing with Drake, are we?'

Clooney colored. 'What do you mean by that?'

'Back then, they wouldn't go to sea

with a female on board. Claimed it brought bad luck, although that was never proved. I'm right impressed to see you haven't developed one inch over three hundred years, mister. Still believe in witches too?'

'Damnit, Morg, a female can cloud a man's thinkin'. You know that; I've heard you say it in the past. Hell burnt it! I've never known you to stick your neck out for any skirt in the years we been together. What's so different about this one?'

Morgan sighed, some of the toughness leaving his face now.

'Later, man, later. First let's see what we're up against.'

'You're the boss, Morg. I'll wait until you're ready to tell me.' Morgan kicked his horse ahead. Clooney called after him: 'But I'll still want to know.'

* * *

Morgan and Clooney studied the scene below. The sights, scents and sounds of rural Mexico filled their senses as a balmy breeze fluffed the clouds overhead and stirred the giant rhododendron bushes that shielded them from sight.

Off to their right a ways, dismounted and sprawled out belly-flat amongst the trees was the most highly dangerous bunch of fighting men to invade Old Mexico from the north in quite a time. They also watched and absorbed the scene in silence.

They were beginning to understand what Morgan already had concluded, namely that this was shaping up to be every bit as big a challenge as they had figured from the outset. Plus.

Valley Moritomo appeared to slumber a little beneath a gentle sun. Stretching some twenty miles from lazy bottom lands in the north to the Sierra foothills in the south, the verdant valley was patchworked with areas of grazing lands interspersed with wide brown fields sown with maize, milo, barley, wheat and corn. And perched atop the rearing hill dominating everything else was what at a distance appeared to be a castle fashioned out of yellow stone: Hacienda St Leque.

Roads, trails, alleyways, bridle-paths and animal-pads criss-crossed the land, fanning out like spokes in a wheel from the whitewashed village which lay some two miles distant from the siege site.

Everywhere the eye fell there was activity. The background music was the ring of a blacksmith's hammer, the rumble of laden wagons, the occasional sharp crack of a blacksnake whip.

The whips were in the hands of the uniformed and mounted overseers, and they cracked viciously just over the heads and bent backs of the army of ragged peasants working in field, mill and mine as far as the eye could see.

That this was anything but an everyday rural scene was plain at a glance. No mercenary had witnessed anything like this since before the war, when slavery fuelled the engines and filled the coffers of the Deep South.

But such men were not easy to shock.

They had been told what to expect down here. If they were surprised at all it was when they recognized the gray-garbed, blackcapped overseers as provincial troopers. The Mexican military might well be notoriously corrupt and cruel but they'd never been known to be this brazen in their criminality.

The impression was formed very quickly that this Colonel Moro they were hearing about was no man to be taken lightly.

'Well, at least they didn't exaggerate about how bad things are down here, Morg,' Buck remarked.

'Tell me something I don't know.'

Morgan was testy; the deep creases in his flat cheeks and the set of his jaw proclaimed it. Although expecting to encounter upheaval on a grand scale, he still hadn't expected things to be this bad. For not only had the military plainly taken over Don Julius's valley, they were running it as an ongoing commercial operation and running it with high efficiency, by the looks.

Plainly the military was stronger than he'd been led to believe, which, he supposed, explained why a man of even Diaz's power and status had succumbed to them.

Or almost succumbed, he corrected himself, eyes drifting again to the hilltop hacienda, which from a distance reminded him more of a medieval castle — under siege, of course.

He knew he would be taking a much closer look at the hacienda situation later, but already he could see that Moro had the place completely surrounded.

'Too tough, you reckon?' asked Buck Clooney.

'Why don't you talk straight, mister?'

'I thought I was.'

Hard gray eyes drilled at the unremarkable face of Buck Clooney. 'What?' he demanded.

'You're makin' a big mistake, Morg. That rich woman ain't for you. OK, Diaz is in a bind now — that's why we're here. But he's still rich as Midas . . . so how you reckon she's gonna tumble for an agein', baldin' mean-tempered gunslinger like yourself? What is it, Morg? You turnin' soft in the head in your old age?'

When push came to shove, Buck Clooney could be as hard as any man.

But still Morgan refused to respond. The man simply turned his broad back and moved across to the horses.

But knew in his heart all the man said was true.

*   *   *

Iselda Diaz was everything Clooney claimed: rich, spoiled, wilful and unscrupulous. She could also act very strange at times, he would concede, but she sure as shooting wasn't loco.

Then he recalled that it wasn't Clooney who'd said that, but Damaron.

He massaged his knuckles, tingling with pleasure as he recollected his fist smashing into the gunslinger's jaw, likely busting it. Then he frowned as he tugged a slip of paper from the breast pocket of his denim shirt. It was the wire Iselda had sent upon seeing his reply to the don. She was eternally grateful, so she said, and had signed it: 'Love, Iselda.'

He wanted to believe she really meant that. He'd assured her he loved her, and he was equally optimistic that he had been speaking from the heart.

After twenty years behind a gun spent evading the trap of love and the iron jaws of matrimony, the gun loner had eventually realized it would all end one day soon, and a man would need someone to be there beside him when he awoke in the middle of the night sweating from some crimson gunsmoke dream.

Morgan shook his big head, reminded himself that even should he prove capable of busting the siege of St Leque, she would still be another man's wife, still the classic, arrogant by-product of the élitist environment that had spawned her.

He shrugged and swung up. He'd fret

about that later. In the meantime he had to go figure out how ten men could overcome a regiment.

'No, stay put,' he ordered as Clooney made to mount also. 'I'll scout out the siege scene alone.'

'Ain't that risky, Morg? You can be sure there's soldier look-outs all over that end of the valley.'

'I'll try and bring you back a dress, mister.'

'Huh?'

Morgan heeled away. 'You're sounding more like someone's maiden aunt every day.'

3

BESIEGED

Moro's sentry found himself a a fine spot from which to peer down upon Don Julius's besieged hacienda, some half-mile distant. This was a secluded, sylvan hollow nestled into the steep flanks of the mountainside. Tall ferns framed the scene, radiant in variegated hues of subtle green. Wild grapes tangled around the tree-trunks and wild violets blossomed in the shade.

Here a small stream burbled from the rocks to form a delicate pool before falling some one hundred feet on to the rocky ledge below.

To this pool all the mountain creatures came. Some, shy and watchful, came only to slake their thirst. Others, stalking and cruel, came to kill and feast then dip their furred faces in the pool to rinse their bloodied mouths.

The soldier sat on a lichened boulder with the stream murmuring in back of him. He focused his field glasses upon the hacienda. The brightly colored pennants of Don Julius fluttered above the stone parapets. The don flew them every day as a gesture of defiance to his enemies.

The sentry placed the glasses carefully beside him, then reached round for his rucksack. For a moment he imagined he glimpsed something moving a short distance off through the brush, but before he could focus his gaze the shadow, or whatever it had been, had disappeared. He turned back for the rucksack.

The dark figure stepped out on to the sun-drenched banks of the clear pool. The man moved soundlessly towards the seated soldier, footsteps absorbed by the moist white sand. The sentry grunted as he twisted round to scratch his rump, heedless of all but his comfort.

Suddenly Morgan stepped in front of the man. He leapt up with a cry, snatching at his belt gun with incredible swiftness. This led Morgan to strike far faster and harder than he'd intended. His gun barrel clipped the man's skull, he went skittering backwards, caught a boot-heel on a root and his body vanished with a rustling sound over the overgrown rim in the swift blink of an eye.

Morgan leaned his rifle against a tree and fumbled with a match to light a cigarette. Whatever he felt for the dead soldier couldn't be read in his face. Clay Morgan had not needed to see the executed peons and farmboys back in the foothills to know exactly how things stood in Moritomo Valley. Down here it was once again a case of kill or be killed and the devil claim the man who faltered or showed one shred of mercy.

He perched on the dead man's rock, picked up the dropped field glasses and took his first clear look at Iselda's home.

Hacienda St Leque was a sight to impress any man, even a hardened veteran of the gun.

The first Don Julius had spared no expense in erecting his hilltop fortress. Fashioned entirely from yellow stone quarried from the Sierras, the sprawling compound had every imaginable defence against attack or invasion.

The complex was entirely surrounded by a moat which had been built at huge cost by engineers who'd based it upon the illustration of an English moated castle supplied by the don. It had gunports in the walls and he glimpsed Gatling guns, squat, dark and menacing, mounted at strategic positions surrounding a half-moon-shaped terrace off on the eastern side.

Yet sturdy, beautiful and well-defended though it well might be, Hacienda St Leque was surrounded.

Morgan didn't need the glasses to pick out the foxholes, trenches and bunkers that encircled this stone castle.

Inside these breastworks and battlements Morgan could detect figures moving about sluggishly, servants carrying out mundane chores.

On the upper levels, however, the scene was dramatically different, and Morgan shook his head in genuine wonder as he peered through his glasses at what was taking place in what appeared to be a fortified courtyard.

Everywhere his gaze fell there were men and women attired in finest silks and satins, mingling and conversing together with every sign of gaiety, only occasionally drifting off to the battlements to gaze up-valley. Liveried servants moved amongst the grandees and there was even a small orchestra playing in the shade of a striped green overhang.

Morgan thrust his hat back and knuckled his eyes.

He might have smiled had he been a smiling kind of man. This was incredible!

As a man who admired courage

above all else, he could not help but be impressed by Don Julius. To flaunt his defiance in the very face of the world outside, to live like a king while his kingdom had been taken away from him and the enemy waited at the gate to cut his throat — surely only a man of great courage, or perhaps a madman, could live like this.

He stiffened.

Two women and a man had just appeared from a darkened archway in a wall that lay bathed in golden sunlight. The man was youthful and bearded, the woman on his arm perhaps even younger with waist-length ebony hair.

And yet it was the second woman who commanded his full attention.

Iselda appeared even more lovely in this opulent setting than she had done back in Arizona.

Although filled with admiration, the mercenary waited for the hit to the heart that did not come. His jaws worked as he watched the woman he wanted to love move across the upper gallery like some graceful, sleek animal, totally assured in her beauty.

He lusted for her, sure. But surely he was meant to feel more than that?

He was diverted from his tumultuous thoughts when he noticed how Iselda kept turning to the younger woman, smiling at her constantly, touching her affectionately upon the shoulder.

It could only be her daughter, Morgan speculated. Even during their brief time together in Arizona, Iselda had spoken of her daughter with such intensity and emotion that he'd found himself growing bored at times. Iselda had made it crystal clear that her daughter was the most important thing in her entire life. He supposed a man should admire such remarkable maternal devotion, and yet he had to ask himself: if Iselda was so besotted by her daughter, where did that leave him?

A short, ramrod figure in black velvet with a mane of silver hair joined the trio and Morgan guessed he was catching his first glimpse of Don Julius Diaz.

Slowly then he lowered the glasses and drew a hand across his forehead.

Emotions warred within him and there was a taste like dust in his throat. Had he expected too much?

Was it Iselda he loved or was it simply the idea of love itself that had infatuated him as he'd found himself staring down the barrel of his lonely middle years?

But Clay Mogan was not the breed of man ever to waste time in soul-searching.

'Get on with the job, man,' he said aloud, hefting the glasses again. 'Do the job, get the woman out of there, then worry whether it all tallies or not.'

This time he focused, not upon the glittering, almost unreal world within the hacienda itself but upon the enemy below. The besiegers. The gray-garbed troops of Colonel Moro lurking and skulking behind their reinforcements, the human carrion-eaters waiting to pick the bones of those handsome indolent people above.

He made a mental note of every position and its strength, then ran the glasses across the valley until at last he found what he was searching for: the dam which held back the tributary of the Rio Abreau some distance upriver from the valley town.

He was no longer thinking of Iselda Diaz. He was focused exclusively on how to get inside the hacienda and the phrase 'diversionary tactics' slipped into his mind from his days in the butternut uniform of the Confederacy.

* * *

Don Julius sipped red wine from a silver goblet.

'You are lovely today, my daughter,' he murmured. 'Ahh, to be so young again.'

'To be young and in love, *Padre*,' said Lucetta, clinging to the arm of Johnny Chavez. She said no more, yet the way she cut a glance from one parent to the other was eloquent enough. That look said plainly: 'So you and Mother would hardly know what I'm talking about, would you?'

The Diazes's only offspring possessed a mean streak and always had done. She'd been born with it, but if the don might be vaguely aware of this trait, his wife was not nor could ever be. Others might contend that the girl whom her parents often referred to as Princess, although undeniably beautiful in a faintly chilly kind of way, was also devious, wilful and at times actually cruel, especially with her tongue.

She owed her beauty to her mother but her temperament was all her father's. Although neither parent would ever admit it, there was a great deal of similarity between the ageing despot and the spoiled child.

But whatever defects the parents might possess, they were forgiven. Wealth and beauty were highly prized here and the Diazes had them in abundance. Other qualities such as character, integrity and piety enjoyed far less currency. The don had set this pattern originally and his sycophants, courtiers and underlings subscribed to it undeviatingly.

A rifle cracked fifty feet above the heads of the quartet now standing beside a table covered by a golden cloth. None even glanced up at the defender who had fired. A war was raging around the fortress, yet it seemed like merely a backdrop to the real business at hand, the business of pleasure, romance and the head-long pursuit of the good life.

In reality however, with the siege now six months old and with no end to it in sight, many amongst the besieged were privately beginning to fear that eventually their idyll must surely come to an end. And what would wealth or beauty or youth be worth if the unthinkable should happen and Moro crossed the drawbridge?

For at last the massive supplies which Diaz had brought in before the enemy circle closed around them were beginning to dwindle. They were losing fighting men every day now. The defenders were low on gunpowder and ammunition and it was growing all too plain that no officialdom cared enough about the arrogant and tyrannical don and his purebred adherents to feel moved to mount a rescue operation.

And still no sign of that saving straw which the Diazes were clinging to so hopefully — the American mercenary, Clay Morgan.

'Still nothing heard of your gringo hero, dearest Mother?' Lucetta remarked acidly as servants brought drinks upon a silver tray.

Iselda made the sign of the cross upon her breast. 'He shall come. He is that sort of man.'

'And just what sort is that, Doña Iselda?' enquired the daughter's young man. Johnny Chavez was something of a mystery at the hacienda. Prior to the troubles, he had suddenly materialized as a young visiting aristocrat about town whose main accomplishments appeared to have been living well with no visible means of support and eventually winning the heart of the don's daughter.

Chavez had been amongst the very last of the valley dwellers to gallop across the drawbridge over the moat on that black day when the defence collapsed and Moro's soldiers overran the valley.

Handsome, personable and assured, Chavez was a favorite with the women of St Leque but still something of a puzzle to many of the men, including Don Julius.

But the don's policy had always been: 'If the Princess wants something she may have it.' And so Johnny Chavez was accepted as the girl's suitor and future husband — even though the family didn't know anything like as much of his background as might have been desired.

'Clay Morgan is a true *hombre*,' Iselda remarked to her audience after a brief silence. The don's face appeared to twitch involuntarily with jealousy at that remark but no one seemed to notice. 'He is big, he is beautiful and it is quite impossible to be in the same room with him without feeling his power.'

'The patron saint of killers,' Lucetta remarked wryly. 'You know, I really hope that this *hombre* manages to make it past the barricades if for no other reason than that I might see for myself just exactly what it is about this *Americano* that has made so deep an impression on you, mother.' She paused, then added; 'Surely you must feel the same, *Padre*?'

Diaz made to reply but stopped as something caught the sun on the mountain slopes and briefly flashed with light.

'The scum scouts are busy today,' he remarked. 'Perhaps they are preparing for another assault?'

'They lost a dozen last time they attacked,' Iselda reminded with some satisfaction. 'I doubt Moro would be eager to lose more so soon.'

'Perhaps the vermin soldiers are so terrified of the great gringo mercenary who is coming that they might try to win victory before he arrives,' said her daughter. She tugged petulantly at her young man's arm. 'Come along, Johnny. I need some excitement.'

'Please do not go, my precious,' Iselda pleaded, hands extended. 'Your mama needs you today.'

'Think gringo, Mama,' the girl called back over her shoulder with a cold laugh. 'That should warm you . . . if he is all that you say.'

Doña Iselda dabbed at her eyes as her daughter's mocking laugh faded. Her full lips moved to the cadence of a strangely mournful chant:

Darkness lies upon the land,
The death seeds have been sown;
The wind has blown our hope away,
And God forgets his own.

She stared forlornly off at the distant Sierras, totally unaware that at that very moment in the hills much closer stood a lone American soldier of fortune, watching her through a dead man's field glasses.

★　★　★

The squat figure of the new master of Valley Moritomo stood in the archway beneath the overgrown bougainvillaea which screened the western side of the long squat stone-and-adobe mansion. He had commandeered the place as his new headquarters and it had become known as Moro's Bunker.

Moro often came to this spot beneath the spreading vine. It was a place where he could be alone with his thoughts. He often studied the bougainvillaea, knew it now in all its changing appearances and moods.

It was a restless vine, alway searching, probing and spreading, never content to remain just as it was.

He felt that the vine yearned to conceal all things in its darkly verdant leaves. It often appeared half-asleep in the mornings, but like the colonel himself, became restless as night approached. The early evening wind caused it to shudder now as though ghostly hands were fanning the leaves.

But as night enveloped the valley and the last fiery glow faded from the distant Sierras, the restlessness left the vine and it was still and silent as it waited for the stars.

Shaking himself from his reverie, Moro moved with sudden new energy along the short pathway to the gate where two uniformed men snapped to attention and clicked polished boot-heels.

Next to the don's barricaded hacienda, the stone mansion was the most heavily guarded dwelling in a hundred miles.

'Reports?' he rapped.

The sentries knew there was but one topic that genuinely interested their commander at the present, namely the rumor that a band of Yankee mercenaries was heading for the province.

Moro's chief intelligence officer had even come up with a name: Morgan. They'd traced the man through regimental files and identified him as one Clay Morgan of Arizona Territory, ex-Confederate Army officer turned mercenary. Clay Morgan sounded exactly like the sort of trouble Colonel Moro could well do without.

The regiment was readying for another attack upon the hacienda but Moro was holding back while squads of scouts scoured the north regions for sign of the Americans.

There was no news from the scouts, so the sentries informed him now. The colonel took heart from this for it was quite some time since he'd first heard the Morgan rumor, yet there was still not a whisper of a sighting of an army of bloodthirsty gringo gunmen. He decided then and there, as a chilly night wind caused the bougainvillaea to whisper and rustle and turn its shimmering leaves to the first stars, that if there was still no hint of alarm come daybreak he would personally lead the attack against the fortress and this time would press on remorselessly until the sturdy doors were breached and they brought him Diaz's head in a sack.

* * *

'Pablo?'

'*Si*?'

'You hear something?'

'Like what?'

'Like the rustle.'

'What rustle, Chino?'

'The rustle in the grass. Do you not hear it?'

'You were asleep so you hear nothing.'

'Asleep at my post? Never! I still hear what I hear. We must look.'

Squat Chino promptly heaved himself off his comfortable bench in the snug watch-house, scooped up a carbine and led the way out on to the dam wall.

The hundred-foot-long dam slung across the Rio Abreau's chief tributary was the centerpiece of Don Julius's elaborate irrigation system. Since its installation a decade earlier it had almost doubled the productivity of the valley. Moro recognized the dam's importance and had ordered it to be guarded round the clock.

The sentries paced dutifully to and fro, peering down upon the earth-packed rock wall which flanked the high earthworks dam on the town side. All was quiet.

Or so it seemed.

Directly below the two figures as they moved slowly along the dam wall, three deadly gunmen lay snake-still in a shadowy grassed hole amongst big boulders: Crazy Jake, Ken Waldo and Dundee.

As usual, young Waldo was afflicted by an itching trigger-finger.

'Let's let 'em have it,' he panted eagerly. 'Just look at 'em up there . . . sittin' ducks. We couldn't miss if they paid us.'

'Hush up!' admonished Dundee, senior man of the group. 'We gotta wait until Morg checks out that buildin' at the far end and makes sure there ain't more sentries than we figure.'

'How long's he gonna take?' whispered Crazy Jake. He too had been lusting for gun action ever since crossing the border.

'He'll take as long as he takes — ' Dundee growled, then cut off abruptly. In turning to speak to Crazy Jake, the veteran of a dozen mercenary jobs made an uncharacteristic mistake when his rifle clicked against a stone. The short, sharp sound carried clearly to the soldiers above and they jumped back from the rim of the dam like startled deer.

Ken Waldo seized the whistle hanging by a lanyard around his neck and blew a blast loud enough to awaken the dead.

4

STRANGE ALLIANCES

Everthing happened at once.

Morgan, Cage and Wilson were belly-wriggling their stealthy way up a gradual slope towards the long dark bulk of the frame-and-adobe building at the eastern end of the wall when the whistle blasted, sounding like the shriek of the devil. Thirty feet away Crazy Jake and Waldo were busily packing fat plugs of dynamite, stolen from the military arms store, against the base of the dam wall.

The long building which Morgan thought resembled a stables, and fervidly hoped it might be, erupted with a sudden rumble of deep-throated sound as the high-pitched shriek of the alarm whistle ripped through the night.

The 'stable' was in fact an improvised

barracks housing men with guns. Moro had foreseen the strategic importance of the dam and had taken full precautions against possible sabotage.

'Judas Priest!' Morgan mouthed as he watched fast-moving soldiers streaming out into the night. But in a flash he was over the rim of the compound and delivering orders to the others in a full bullhorn roar.

'Take them down!'

They stared back at him wild-eyed but didn't move — frozen by the unexpected moment. 'I said cut loose, you chittle-wits!' he raged, jerking up twin guns. 'It's too damn late to run!'

They were pros and every man jolted out of his uncharacteristic moment of shock within the next heartbeat.

Instantly the dam wall was lighted up by fierce yellow tongues of gunflame that lanced up the slope to chop down running figures like so many skittles.

Jolted by the fierceness of that first vicious volley, the troopers began to panic. Sensing this, the mercenaries found all the encouragement needed to press home their advantage.

Morgan showed the way. His sixguns roared three times and and two men went down hard, kicking at the earth, dying.

The third man, however, retaliated with a swath of yammering rifle fire. Morgan hurled himself flat with death whistling over him. Lightning-fast, Cage and Wilson homed in on the rifleman and blew him off the wall in one murderous hailstorm of flying lead.

Next moment Cage buckled violently and hit the ground. The troopers were fanning out and fighting back by this. The minute that followed was as hair-raising as any in Morgan's vast experience. Men were dropping on either side, but despite the Mexicans' gritty fight-back, the superior teamwork and gunskill of the mercenaries saw them gradually driven back until at last they were pushed as far as the dam's edge. Then Morgan gave the order to charge and every man responded, following him upslope at the run, howling like savages.

Charging up that blood-soaked strip, Morgan was no longer a thinking, reasoning man and more like some kind of fighting machine. His mind switched off to be replaced by killer instincts honed over a twenty-year span of living by the gun.

He had experienced this same sense of invincibility and immortality previously on the bloody battlegrounds of the South, would doubtless count these moments in the same mold — if he survived Valley Moritomo.

He was flanked on either side by veterans who were experiencing the same exaltation.

There were no such ruthless fighting machines within the ranks of the colonel's men.

The troopers were simply trying to do their jobs as best they might, and on this murderous stretch of Mexican battlefield that simply was not enough.

Bullets peppered the walls as Morgan

reached the barracks. He spun around and snapped a lightning shot at the figure running for the building's doorway. The youthful trooper staggered sideways as lead punched his head askew and hurled him out of sight.

Morgan didn't see the man fall as he swiveled his gaze in the opposite direction to see a half-dozen menacing figures rushing his way. Chanting.

He dived headlong through the barracks' doorway with hot lead searching for him. He rolled to his feet and backed up away from the rectangle of the entrance, reloading his right-hand cutter with feverish haste. The pale wash of faint dawn light silhouetted the figures of the *bravos* jostling one another in their eagerness to be the first inside to claim the scalp of the 'big gringo.'

A fusillade of shots pumping with machine-gun rapidity from two American Colt revolvers welcomed the trio, and even after the last blood-spurting soldier had fallen backwards and gone down under that ferocious volley, Morgan kept triggering until gun hammers clicked upon empty shell-casings.

Only then did he begin breathing again. Broad shoulders sagged. The air was thick with choking gunsmoke. His gunsmoke. The place also smelt sharply of death and unwashed bodies. Slowly, fumblingly, he reloaded, his barrel chest heaving from exertion.

It was growing quiet outside. Then: 'Morg?'

'I'm all right,' he replied, and as he walked for the door he reeled from a shuddering, reverberating thunderclap. He emerged from the barracks in time to see the entire mid section of the dam rising some thirty to forty feet into the air with a billowing, surging fireball beneath it.

The awful roar of the dynamite reached him and deadened his eardrums as he dived away with a torrent of floodwater rushing unimpeded through the yawn-ing gap in the wall as those mercenaries who'd survived stormed away to be swallowed by the woods.

★ ★ ★

The fragrant smoke of the first cigar of the new day trickled from Morgan's lips.

The sky was gunmetal gray and light had begun to filter down off reinforced walls of the hacienda to probe the shadowy places beneath. Setting his CSA Army issue field glasses to his eyes he played his gaze over several empty enemy bunkers and glimpsed gray-garbed figures skulking off through the brush in the direction of the valley town.

'Strategic diversionary tactics,' he said with some satisfaction as he passed the instrument to Clooney. 'Guess they worked for us again.'

Clooney studied his face soberly for a long moment but said nothing. He knew Morgan's tactics of the night had come at a cost. They'd lost three men back at the dam.

Clooney set the glasses to his eyes and focused on the building above them which from this angle looked more like a yellowstone fortress and less like a graceful hacienda. The entire structure was abuzz with movement and sound as the besieged defenders rushed to the balustrades to stare off towards the town, still unable to figure what exactly was going on down there at valley's end.

Morgan stepped from the cover of the trees, raised a Colt and blasted three shots into the dawn sky.

'Morgan!' he roared at the top of his lungs. 'Bring down the bridge! They're running now but that could change any minute! So get moving!'

Confused faces peered down upon his solitary figure with the smoking gun. Long moments of confusion and uncertainty followed above until Morgan clearly heard the woman's cry rise above the murmuring voices.

'It is him! I told you he would come.'

A white arm waved. 'Clay, oh Clay, thank God!'

Morgan just nodded his head impatiently. The veteran was acutely aware of the danger of a counter-attack from a numerically superior foe.

He allowed himself to relax some when after maybe a full minute of further confusion and argument above, they heard the groan of heavy machinery, a vast creaking of timbers, and the two-ton drawbridge tilted slowly away from the wall to be lowered upon its heavy chains before thudding down upon the buttresses on the mercenaries' side of the water.

Clay Morgan led his men upwards and into the unreality of Hacienda St Leque.

★   ★   ★

Freshly shaved, bathed and decked out in fresh, borrowed rig, Morgan towered over his host as he was formally presented.

'*Hombre*!' Don Julius greeted, his aristocratically saturnine features wreathed in smiles as the two men shook hands. 'Señor Morgan . . . or may I address you as Clay as I feel that already you are my most valued friend! Welcome to Hacienda St Leque. Welcome to my family. You already know my lady wife . . . and this is our precious daughter, Lucetta.'

Morgan glanced at the striking, cold-eyed younger woman and nodded. The 'Princess' did not acknowledge the introduction. Morgan cocked a quizzical eyebrow at Iselda Diaz, who shrugged.

'I very much fear it is how the wise man says.' She smiled. 'No man can be a hero to all.'

'But this man is surely the hero of all heroes, woman,' protested the don. 'What courage, what inventiveness! A handful of brave *Americanos* proving able to divert the enemy from our walls long enough to join us? If this is not worthy of the highest praise then I — '

'If you will but open your eyes, *Padre*,' the stately younger woman cut in, 'you will note that, for all the heroism of Mother's special friend and your new hero, we all of us are still prisoners and the look-outs have just reported sighting the enemy returning to besiege us.'

Faces turned to Morgan to see how he would react to this. He did not. He was staring at the stately Iselda Diaz with an expression none could read, with a strange feeling inside that not even he could understand at that moment.

At that moment, the man who had accepted a deadly mission in the name of what he hoped might be love, was experiencing a sudden grave feeling of misgiving and doubt somewhere in the pit of his guts.

No one seemed to notice, particularly not the don, who was in full charge as he led the party through on to the private balcony which opened into a drawing-room. Morgan had never encountered anything as beautiful and luxurious as this besieged hacienda-cum-fortress. Its opulence astounded him, and yet it was also sobering. Seeing Iselda here in her natural surroundings for the first time, pampered by servants and fêted by the don's court — it made him wonder whether a rough-hewn man of the gun could ever hope to lure her away.

Maybe Buck was right. Maybe he was a fool to think a woman of her class could ever love him. And he knew in that jolting moment of self-understanding that it had been love — or the desperate search for it as he faced the onset of his middle age — that had been the motivating factor in responding to Iselda Diaz's desperate plea for help, not money or glory or a lifetime's hunger for adventure. He'd come here with the double intention of saving Iselda Diaz's life, then claiming her as his own.

'Clay, *hombre*, are you all right?'

Iselda's voice jolted him out of it. A

brooding scowl cut his brows. It was surely no time to think of such matters right now. Not with far more pressing issues at hand, it wasn't. Issues, such as how to vanquish Moro, not merely set him running as they had done earlier. He had to concentrate on how to free St Leque and Valley Moritomo totally from its long oppression.

From the windows Morgan saw that the floodwaters had greatly subsided and the distant town was beginning to return to normal. He studied the dam, now with that gaping hole in its wall where Buck Clooney's dynamite had done its destructive work.

Through field glasses he played his vision over the muddied streets of the town, Ascencion, where peons moved to and fro dragging sandbags, furniture and crates. Gray-tunicked troopers moved amongst them, bawling orders. His sweep didn't overlook the unit of cavalry moving purposefully up from the regimental headquarters towards the hacienda. There were maybe thirty men in the group and there surely would be more to support them as soon as the flood crisis was over.

'I sense you would have made a fine general, Señor Morgan,' gushed Diaz, more comfortable now with the formal mode of address. 'From the daring manner in which you were able to secure access here where our enemies have failed for so long, that is.'

'Getting in here might prove the easy part in the long run, like your daughter reckons,' Morgan responded. 'I might as well level. So far I don't have much worked out in the way of plans for getting you and your folks out of here.'

'What you achieved assures me there is no limit to your capabilities,' said Diaz. 'Do you not agree, Iselda?'

The handsome *dama* familiarly linked her arm through Morgan's.

'I realized from the first moment I saw you in Arizona that time, that you were a man who could do anything, Clay.'

Morgan glanced at Diaz. Did the

man know? he wondered. About them? He sensed that maybe the daughter did, or at least had her suspicions. She certainly had something chewing on her pretty liver, that one.

'Maybe it's time we sat down and mapped out our plan to get you out of here,' he suggested.

'Tomorrow,' replied the don. 'Today you heroes must rest and tonight you will be our guests of honor at the banquet. Iselda, you will see to it that this shall be the greatest occasion we have ever celebrated.'

Iselda gave her assurance before turning back to Morgan. He had been absently studying Lucetta, who stood at the center of a small group out on the balcony. 'Is she not truly beautiful?' the woman gushed. Next instant, sudden tears sprang to her eyes. 'You will save her, won't you, Clay?'

'I'm fixing to try and save you all. That's what I'm here for, Iselda.'

'Indeed it is,' agreed the don.

But Iselda gripped the gunfighter's

arm and forced him to meet her gaze. She was fiercely intense. 'You must promise me here and now, upon this very spot where we stand, that whatever else you do you will save my precious princess. Promise me, Clay, you must promise me!'

Morgan stared down at her, seeing plainly in her face now the signs of the torment she must have suffered in these months of captivity. He imagined he saw desperation in her eyes and wondered what she might be seeing in his. For from the moment their eyes had first met, he knew something had changed between them. He had accepted this mission solely in order to meet Iselda Diaz again in the desperate hope that he might find there that which a lonely, aging mercenary might turn into something solid and significant in his life, something that might anchor him down, fulfil him, perhaps.

He still could not see that prospect.

What he did see was a lovely woman weakened by fear and circumstance who was clinging to him like a frightened child.

He smiled at her with grim reassurance. 'Yeah, I'll save your daughter, Iselda.' He meant it. He never lied.

★ ★ ★

A sense of unreality crowded in on Morgan as he took his place of honor at the don's right hand at the banquet.

The fifty-foot oaken table was adorned with an array of crystal and silver that glittered beneath the brilliant light of three massive chandeliers. Every chair was occupied by a man or woman whose splendid attire would not have been out of place at a first night at the opera in New York or Paris. Servants bustled amongst the guests and a string quartet played in the corner, struggling to make itself heard above the hum of excited voices.

This was a fortress under siege?

He stared directly across the table at Iselda but her back was turned to him. All her attention was focused upon her daughter who, heedless of her mother's devoted eye, chatted animatedly with young Johnny Chavez, the man Morgan understood to be the girl's suitor.

Chavez met his gaze and winked. A hoodlum, Morgan thought, but a tough one if he was any judge. No amount of good manners and style could conceal that fact from the gunmaster's experienced eye. He knew the breed too well. In another setting, in different circumstances, Johnny Chavez could be another Flash Damaron.

For just a moment an image of the gunfighter from Arizona flickered into his mind. Of course it wasn't over between them, he knew. He'd even covertly maintained a watch on their back trail during the journey south, half-expecting to sight a couple of riders tracking their sign. He had little doubt that by the time Damaron recovered from the busted jaw he'd handed him, he'd be set on crossing the Rio to even scores. That dude would never be able simply to let it go.

His breed was too proud, too prickly and just too damn fast with a .45 not to make a try at evening scores.

He flicked his gaze down the length of the table. His riders had duded themselves up handsomely for the grand occasion. Soon there were speeches and cheering and toasts following one after the other and all directed at the gringo heroes of the hour. Nobody mentioned the 'solution'; not tonight. It seemed to be taken for granted amongst the former lords and masters of Valley Moritomo that such was the impression of decisiveness created by the bunch's besting of Moro in their first bloody encounter, it would only be a matter of time now before they would see the siege raised, the colonel whipped like the cur he was and the valley returned to its rightful overlords, namely the don and his kin.

Morgan only wished he felt so sure.

But such weighty matters could wait until tomorrow, he told himself, beginning at last to feel the benefit of a truly superb moselle.

Tonight he meant to enjoy himself. A man was a long time dead. Three of his riders had gone to their Maker just today. It was quite possible he might join them before another day had passed. He'd always believed he would die violently despite his unrealistic visions of retirement, true love and peaceful days — all those impossible things no man of the guns ever got to enjoy — just the dream.

He was hoping that this one night at least might prove rich and fulfilling as his eye fell on the lovely, troubled face of the don's wife.

★ ★ ★

'We must do something, Johnny.'

'There is nothing we can do, Lucetta.'

'But these mercenaries are our enemies.'

'Possibly not so great an enemy as

the colonel, *chiquita*.'

'But they crushed Moro yesterday.'

'Hurt, not crushed. Look, you can count as well as I, Lucetta. There are fewer than a dozen of these gringo killers left now, yet Moro still has a large part of a regiment left.'

Johnny Chavez paused to shake his dark head of curls.

'No, this Morgan may be *muy macho* but he will never defeat Moro. So, the best thing for us to do is simply sit and wait. Let Morgan lead his butchers against the colonel. Let him kill as many soldiers as he can. In the end he will surely be slain, for the poor fool wants to play the hero and save your mother, and that will surely lead to his death. But the killing he does before he dies will greatly help our cause. For after Moro's ranks have been thinned we shall surely rise and lead the peons to victory over the oppressors.'

Lucetta Diaz's dark eyes glowed with a light others seldom saw.

'I love it when you speak of the

cause, *hombrecito*.' Her expression suddenly altered, turning darker with a hint of malevolence. 'How I despise those like Moro and my father who build their kingdoms on the blood and sweat of the poor! You shall never know how grateful I am that you came into my life and taught me just how wrong such things are. Suddenly I saw the injustice, the cruelty and the obscenity of our way of life.'

'You were an unexpected convert, Lucetta. But now I do believe you are even more fervid than myself in your hunger to see the rule of the bloody-handed *ricos* smashed here and Valley Moritomo returned once and for all to its rightful owners, the poor. But tell me. Do you never regret that our cause sets you against your own family?'

'My father is the most selfish man in all Sonora and my mother is sick in the mind!'

'But she loves you.'

'I do not seek love, Johnny, only justice.' She smiled at him, almost too brightly. 'And, of course, I seek your love for me. You do love me truly, don't you, Johnny?'

'Do the stars love the sky?'

She kissed him. 'Now . . . tell me, Johnny. Tell me again how it will be in the valley when my father has been driven out and the evil Moro is no more. I love to listen when you speak of the peons' revolt. Describe for me how the oppressors will suffer. That is the part I love hearing best.'

Johnny Chavez studied the animated face of the woman he professed to love. There was more to the handsome young man than anybody guessed, none of it good. For he was infinitely more dangerous and capable than he appeared, and treacherous in a way so far unsuspected in St Leque. He spoke of freedom and equality for the shirtless ones, yet dreamed only of personal power and glory while assisting the poor to dismiss the powerful and the rich. In the end, he knew, he would be filling the oppressors' shoes himself.

He had seen such things happen and would stop at nothing in his ambition. Yet treacherous and deadly though he undoubtedly was, he still half-suspected that he must appear as almost soft-centered alongside his Princess.

Lucetta was genuinely looking forward to the demise of her own parents, which impressed him greatly. She had taken to a dream of bloody revolution the way a puppy dreams of a warm hearth. The don's daughter had become a key player in Chavez's far-reaching plans and would continue to be so for as long as she proved valuable: until Valley Moritomo belonged to himself and his band of ragged *bandidos*, who, posing as revolutionaries and idealists, were crowned the new despots of the 'kingdom.'

Then it would be goodbye, Lucetta — the long goodbye. He genuinely admired his fianceé's beauty, temperament and strength. But those qualities would not save her in the end. For what man in his right mind would ever be fool enough to trust any girl he knew to be crazy, dangerous and simply no damned good?

★　★　★

The narrow street echoed with cheering. The sounds of acclaim were loud but lacked sincerity. The madame of the bordello, who had grown fat and lazy over the years, waddled to a window. She threw up her hands.

'It is the colonel's carriage. How wonderful! Girls!'

It was early morning and the half-naked girls were exhausted and uninterested. Even so, they joined fat Mama at the window and blew kisses and forced smiles as the splendid rig rolled by.

Moro, ignored the acclaim and slapped his driver over the head with his quirt when the unfortunate man failed to avoid a wide puddle left over from the burst dam. The waters had eventually entered the town itself but without enough volume or force left to cause anything much more than an inconvenience.

Sentries snapped to attention as the rig rolled to a halt before the colonel's headquarters. The squat adobe building had been the *cura*'s house until Moro came to the valley to take over command of his siege. The *cura* now slept and ate in the vestry of the squat little steepled church next door. When the good man of the cloth slept at all, that was.

Moro hated his quarters, the village, the peons and the fact that a man of his culture, breeding and ambition should be forced to endure this Gomorrah out here fifty miles from Santo Niño City and all its sophisticated delights.

He had constantly to remind himself that down-at-heel Ascension could, in time, reward him with all the things he craved. By the time he had finally crushed Hacienda St Leque and assumed authority over both it and the whole valley he would quickly become an excolonel of the military and be well on his way to the position he craved, Provincial Governor.

He was vaguely aware that his lieutenant appeared unusually pale as he stamped inside to fling open the door of his inner sanctum, only to find himself confronting a pair of strange American gunslingers who were both smiling a welcome and covering him with naked sixguns.

The colonel turned brick-red with rage and made to shout, would have done so had not the more dangerous-looking of the intruders touched his brow with his .45 and calmly waved him to his desk chair with the piece.

'Relax, Colonel,' the stranger said smoothly, spinning the weapon on his trigger-finger, then slipping it back into the holster. 'Damaron's the name, this here is Parlee Wilson and this could work out to be about the luckiest day you've ever had. You see, we've traveled a whole mess of miles to catch up with you and this here tinpot war you're having, and to tell you your troubles are as good as over.'

'*Madre de Dios*! I shall have the flesh flayed from your stinking gringo bones and your *cojones* hung upon the highest — '

Moro's words cut off as though a switch had been thrown when hard-faced Parlee deliberately dry-clicked the hammer of his Frontier Model Colt at him. Before the man could recover either balance or dignity, Damaron was talking with the fluency of a Southern Baptist preacherman stoked high on home-stilled gin and preaching to the converted.

The gringo *pistoleros* knew both Clay Morgan and his *renegados* personally, so the pale-jawed Moro was informed. Had fought alongside the bunch once but now were pitted against them. As Damaron spoke he occasionally paused to massage his badly set jaw which no longer quite functioned as it should and had eroded the good looks for which he had been renowned.

Damaron quickly shed both his big smile and his diplomatic manner as he revealed that he had just traveled a hundred Mexican miles on Morgan's trail and would not leave Valley Moritomo until he'd seen the half starved village hounds publicly rip the heart and bowels out of the corpses of all the mercenaries now encamped with the colonel's enemies up at the hacienda.

Surely it would be in the 'great' Colonel Moro's interests to enlist the services of two *pistoleros* of great renown who intimately understood the mercenaries' intentions, tactics, their strengths and weaknesses? Particularly in light of the fact that Morgan had already destroyed Moro's dam, made the great man look a fool, and in Damaron's professional opinion, might very well galvanize Diaz's forces to such an extent that the colonel might eventually be driven from the valley?

While searching for his response

Moro was pricked by an unpleasant thought.

'While I consider your proposal, you should know that the hacienda strength has already been very recently increased by the presence of a band of your countrymen . . . *pistoleros* from Arizona who — '

'Hell, we already know that,' Damaron interrupted with a glitter in his eye. He shrugged dismissively. 'OK, so he's given you some grief. But don't sweat, Colonel. Morgan's just a plodder while I'm the smartest strategist and operator you've ever clapped eyes on. You shake hands with me and I'll show you the right way to use what strength you've already got right here in the valley to bring those yeller walls down and that bunch of tenth-rate would-bes with it. Trust me.'

It was quiet for a long minute as Moro sat staring at the *Americanos*. The silence was thick with uncertainty as jittery staffers peered anxiously round his door.

An outward picture of lazy confidence, Damaron nevertheless positioned himself in a far corner with his right hand around his gunbutt, ready and able to take out Moro and maybe a good dozen of his unimpressive-looking troopers should the Colonel's answer prove to be no.

It was only when Moro at last snapped his fingers and bawled at a lieutenant to pour three large brandies that Damaron let go of the Colt, dropped into a chair and hooked one leg over an armrest. He smiled crookedly; it was the only way he was able to smile now.

'You won't regret this decision, Colonel.'

'I don't intend to.'

5

LOVE AND WAR

Three in the morning and still not tired!

Morgan poured another whiskey as Buck Clooney rolled a fresh cigarette and set it alight. The others had long since retired to their quarters and the two Americans were now alone, sitting on an open balcony. Their conversation had roamed far afield, from Moro and the hacienda to their early days and such disparate topics as love, the fighting man's life, and whether or not there was life after death.

The distant town was quiet. The footfalls of pacing sentries were the only sounds disturbing the silence. Suddenly a door creaked. The two grabbed gunbutts as a manservant appeared on soft-soled shoes.

The man bowed solemnly and turned to Morgan. 'The doña wishes to speak with you, *señor*.'

Morgan's hand slid off his gun handle. 'Now?'

'If you would be so good, *señor*.'

Morgan avoided Clooney's quizzical stare as he rose from his bench to trail the manservant across the courtyard toward the main building.

Striding the echoing corridor behind the man, Morgan felt his heart begin to trot. He didn't know whether it was lust or love stirring within him. How could he know? Love had always been a stranger to him.

The man led him to the darkened west wing and halted before a door where a glimmer of light showed beneath. The servant bowed again then moved soundlessly away down along the corridor.

Morgan watched the man disappear before he opened the door and stepped through.

She was seated in a four-poster bed,

the light from the lamp spilling across her. Raven tresses fell about naked shoulders.

She held out her arms, not speaking. He went to her willingly and heedlessly as a bull charging upon the matador's deadly sword.

Now he was sure it was love.

Surely nothing this good could be anything else?

And reassured by this thought, Morgan found himself seeing everything in a far more positive light. Sure, the odds were still huge. But he'd seen how things were shaping in the valley and had felt Old Man Death's cold breath on the back of his neck several times already here.

So what?

He had bucked the odds all his life, and won. Now he had more reason to fight and win than ever. His mind buzzed with new plans of strategies against the enemy as he gusted blue cigarette smoke up around the the four-poster's ornate canopy and Iselda's naked arm stretched across his deep chest.

'Are you not sorry, Clay?'

'For what?'

'For allowing me to lure you to Mexico?'

'Do I look sorry?'

'You do love me then?'

'You know it.' He spoke with a deep-voiced conviction which for some strange reason he suddenly seemed to question.

What was wrong with him? He had known from the outset that he'd have never taken up the Mexican contract had it not involved this woman at his side. She was proving as warm and loving as he could have hoped, yet as before there was that niggle of doubt. For instance: had she wanted him or his guns? Would he have received that loving letter from her had not this rich glittering life she had made for herself seemed to be teetering on the brink of an abyss?

She rose on one elbow. 'Then if you love me as you say, *caballero*, will you prove it?'

'I thought I just did.'

'I am a selfish and demanding woman, *mi carazón*. I always want more than others can give.'

'Try me.'

'A promise?'

Again he felt a prickle of uncertainty in that oddly disturbing note in her voice, the expression in the eyes that raised the spectre of . . . what? Don't torment yourself, gunfighter. She is sincere . . . if you are. That brought a tightening of his jaw muscles as it must have to any man who was doubting his own emotions.

'What?' he grunted.

'You must promise to save her, no matter what.'

'Her?'

'The princess.'

'Well . . . hell, sure I will. I mean to save every man and woman in this place if I shoot straight and my luck holds good — '

'We must be honest with each other, Clay.' Her expression was sober now, her voice had an edge to it. 'Saving a single soul from this hell would prove a giant task, much less saving everybody. Moro will never allow us to escape. It would destroy his plans and hold him up to ridicule. But the lives of the others, my husband's and even my own life are trivial and unimportant. But my precious Lucetta is pure and untainted and simply must be allowed to live. That is the reason I brought you here — not for anybody else but for her, that you might somehow spirit her away with your great strength and . . . Clay, why are you staring at me so strangely?'

He knew he was doing it. He also knew why.

This loving, obsessive woman wasn't making sense.

'Iselda,' he said, sitting upright, 'I guess I can understand how you feel about your girl. I never had a child of my own, though I hope to one day. But I didn't come here on account of her or Diaz or anybody else. I came here for you. I will get you out of this hell-hole, you can make book on that — '

'No, Clay. You see, I am prepared for Eternity. Perhaps it is the Saviour's will that my sinful life should end this way. I don't care. My life has been over for a long time. I've lived half my life with a man I detest and am surrounded by people as avaricious and cruel as he is. I have no religion left in me. I do not love the poor, do not love anyone, not even God. I love only Lucetta. She is the one person who has made all this pain tolerable.'

His face was granite.

'I figured . . . thought you loved me?'

'But of course I do, *caballero*. But you do not need help or protection or a mother's love. You are the strongest and most invincible *hombre* anybody has ever seen.' Her hand tugged at his powerful arm. '*Por favor*, say you will carry my precious child away from this place no matter what befalls the rest of us. That is the only way I can atone for my sin of bringing such sweet innocence into so wicked a world and

106

leading her into this . . . this hell on earth.'

She rose quickly from the great bed, both arms outstretched as she moved towards an empty corner, as though she could see someone there.

'Princess, run to your mama. She will protect you against the phantoms and devils. Here is my breast. Suckle and sleep while Clay our hero prepares to save you, my dearest *bambina* . . . '

As the rambling voice continued, a slow, cold sensation crept over Morgan's flesh. He stared at the woman's lovely smooth back and seemed to hear the distant laughter of dark gods mocking him for daring to believe he might have found the one thing that had always escaped him in the arms of this sad, bewitching woman.

He was swinging bare feet to the floor when there came a sound like a dragon clearing its throat followed by a long, low whistling noise. Then he heard the crashing roar of falling masonry as the lower east wing of the hacienda took the full impact of a cannon ball hurled from the slopes above.

★   ★   ★

The blast, which blew a wagon-sized hole out of the wall above the moat, was the opening salvo of a savage assault planned by Moro to terminate the bloody siege of Hacienda St Leque.

Overnight, and acting upon the advice of his impressive new gringo henchmen, Colonel Moro had dispatched his only remaining piece of heavy artillery up the rugged Sierra trail, hauled by thirty mules and accompanied by a twenty-man squad of grenadiers under the command of a vengeance-hungry Flash Damaron.

Damaron had convinced the Colonel that his missions with Morgan had made him expert in the unexpected. The bullet in the back or the unexpected tactic were all part of

Morgan's stock in trade, and consequently his.

He pointed out that Moro had a cannon, which had thus far proved relatively ineffective. What was plainly needed here was to set the cannon up where it might prove totally unexpected and strategically triumphant.

While the cannon made its four-hour journey the full force of the regiment was armed, briefed and dispatched to the hacienda.

The cannon's opening salvo was the signal for the encircling troops to attack. They opened up with a barrage of rifle fire, grenades and lighted sticks of dynamite which were hurled like bombs across the moat.

The regiment fought like men possessed, the way fighting men mostly will when threatened with death by firing-squad should they fail in their designated objective.

Moro left no doubt in any man's mind what that objective was, precisely. The hacienda was to be taken with Don

Julius's head presented to him in a sack. He would settle for nothing less.

The tactics and assault might have succeeded, should have done so had it not been for the mercenaries. This was exactly the kind of hell-for-breakfast situation Morgan's men thrived on. They knew exactly how to respond and did so murderously well. Under the lash of Morgan's tongue they raked the enemy ranks with deadly rifle fire from the high walls, tricked him into making foolish moves, then rained burning pitch and masonry down upon those who ventured too close to the moat.

But each time it seemed as though the defence was achieving mastery another mighty bellow of sound erupted from higher up, followed by the splintering crash of a shell smashing through timber and stone.

A harried Don Julius at first suspected that Morgan might be showing yellow when he came to him with his 'plan' to deal with the damaging cannon. Quit the castle and take the cannon out of the equation? How in the name of the Holy Father did the gringo gunman imagine he could do that?

Morgan told him. Iselda had informed him of the secret escape tunnel on the hacienda's southern side. Morgan's plan was to take a handful of his best men, quit the siege, make his way up to the cannon site, and take the damaging weapon out of the battle equation with a surprise attack. Simple.

'Impossible!' was the don's reaction. But Iselda was there and her response was totally opposite. 'Give the man the keys to the tunnel and take a brandy for your courage, Don Julius!'

An hour later found Morgan, Clooney, Reno, Smith and Ken Waldo 500 feet above the battleground and stealthily closing in on the cannon emplacement.

As they closed in upon the unsuspecting enemy, Morgan suddenly jolted to a halt with an exclamation of astonishment. His eyes snapped wide as the moonlight picked out the animated face of an American he'd last seen crashing to the floor of an Arizonan saloon under the smash of his fist.

'Ready . . . aim . . . ' Damaron bawled to the figures crouched about the cannon, for this had been his concept and up to that moment he'd pursued it with murderous success.

Up to that moment . . .

'Fire!' Morgan breathed and his pistol shot hit Damaron hard, sent him spinning away into the surrounding brush to crash from sight.

Instantly the mercenaries loosed a withering barrage that had men tumbling like ninepins, falling away, threshing and dying as nimble hands loosened wheel-cocks, powerful shoulders were put to the wheel and a 90-bore cannon rocked forwards to smash its way through a screen of small trees before beginning its tumultuous descent down the hillside.

It was all over in mere moments. The mercenaries had done what they'd set out to do. But they'd already lost one man, two others were wounded — and now enemy reinforcements were quitting the siege and climbing the steep slope.

'Let's go!' bawled Morgan, with a bleeding Reno slung over one shoulder. The snarling guns of Waldo and Clooney covered their retreat.

With the cannon removed from the attack, the defenders at the hacienda took fresh heart and stepped up their withering fire on the encircling enemy below. Some of the heart appeared to leave the gray ranks of the attackers and eventually the defenders were emboldened to drop the drawbridge across the moat, enabling a sortie to clatter across and overrun the nearest enemy dugout where bloody slaughter was achieved before the lightning retreat.

The results of succeeding sorties ranged from costly on one account to devastating on others.

At one late stage a four-man squad of defenders and mercenaries almost overran the outpost from which an enraged Colonel Moro was personally rallying the troops in the wake of Damaron's failure and the devastating loss of his precious cannon.

The result was two mercenaries dead, the hacienda counter-attack first faltering then retreating across the quickly raised drawbridge — a return almost to the grim status quo but for the dead and wounded on either side of this war of attrition.

Morgan lighted a cigar and stared down bleakly at the yellow spurts of gunfire in the night. He was telling himself that there could be but one end to this siege if they gave up on the notion of quitting the fortress again and striking a crushing blow to the foe. Dundee fetched him a double whiskey but he brushed it aside with a grunt. He was exhausted, bitter and already sensed his southern mission had been a mistake from start to end. But, being Morgan, that only made him that much more committed to turning the whole thing around and coming out on top — if just for the hell of it.

* ★ *

The killer just could not believe it. A busted arm, a bullet in his hip and a body covered in cuts and bruises from his fall — and he was to be punished! Surely Moro was simply letting off steam when he came swinging into the infirmary confirming his earlier orders that his officer in charge was to have the gringos ready for immediate transportation to Rio Toro prison?

'You can't do this — ' the gunfighter began, but cut off as a lead-tipped swagger-stick slashed across his face and knocked him off the bloodstained bunk.

'Stinking gringo!' Moro raged. 'I was a fool to believe you might be — '

That was as far as he got. Damaron heaved his crippled body off of the floor and attacked him fiercely, breaking his nose and ripping off half an ear with his teeth until the combined weight of four militiamen beat him unconscious to the floor.

Panting and bloodied, the men stepped back, fully anticipating the gunfighter's instant execution. But after ten full seconds standing over Damaron with a cocked pistol aimed at his head, the colonel shivered, lowered the weapon and stepped back.

'No . . . that would be too easy,' he panted. 'Five years in Rio Toro will be at least five times worse than being killed! Take them away!'

Colonel Moro felt a little better as he took himself outside to calm down. But when he stared across at the lights of the hacienda in the night he was suddenly feeling angry all over once more as he strode off to lead the next assault personally.

★   ★   ★

Morgan said, 'It's got to be done.'

'It is crazy,' Diaz insisted. 'You will throw your lives away on this bravado mission, and with your *compañneros* leaderless they too shall fall and splendid St Leque will be doomed.'

'It's five days since the battle with the cannon and we're no further ahead,' Morgan stated flatly. 'I'm not a patient man, Don Julius, and I'm not about to stand around up here taking pot-shots or hustling across the moat for ten minutes to stir them up before running back with our tails between our legs, then sitting down again to watch our supplies being slowly eaten away. I'm staging a bust-out and I'm going to take Moro out of this game or I won't be coming back. What's more, I'll do it tonight on account of there's no moon. I want you to throw a big shindig with music and hoopla to cover us and lull them into thinking nothing special is happening up here.'

He paused to glance directly across the elaborate table-setting at Iselda. He had realized early that their love, or whatever it had been, was now just a memory. But he cared for her still, was prepared to take chances for her which he might not for another. He nodded firmly, reassuringly.

'I'll succeed. Then you will have what you want.'

'*Muches gracias, hombrecito,*' the woman said tearfully, gratefully. 'I knew I could count on you.'

Morgan swung on his heel and quit the little group gathered around the don's glittering table.

No one noticed the slender figure of Lucetta listening and watching from the shadows of the passageway just outside. She waited for Morgan's powerful figure to disappear from sight then slipped away in the direction of Johnny Chavez's quarters.

6

COME FILL THE GRAVES

Alone on a parapet above the north wing Morgan watched the new day unfold.

He knew it must be the day. His day. Death or glory.

Before dawn tomorrow he knew he'd either have regained the initiative in this war or he would be dead. For the reality of the situation was that, despite earlier successes, the hacienda had been bottled up for four costly days by Moro's onslaughts and there were now increasing signs that the enemy was preparing another full-scale attack.

Tobacco smoke curled around his expressionless features but behind the mask the mercenary captain felt the tightness that always came when he knew he was readying to risk his life again.

He believed he had no choice. Men like Buck, Waldo, Dundee and Chiller would follow him anyplace, partly because they were addicted to danger and partly because of their trust in him both to lead and win.

Having already lost more good men than he could afford he was ready to quit the hacienda tonight afoot with just one man, thread his way through enemy lines, cross the river at a spot where the defences were sparse and then go after his man.

One man dead could change it all around.

Tonight it would be him or Moro — winner take all.

★　★　★

Twilight.

It was that long moment before the frogs began to croak in the slow, winding river, when superstitious Mexican women drew their *rebozos* across their mouths to keep out the evil vapors of the night air. The old women believed the early evening air was defiling and brought evil to all who breathed it.

In the dusty blue dusk of Valley Moritomo the rearing bulk of Hacienda St Leque was beginning to twinkle with lights. Upon the upper parapets and walkways sentries paced out their vigil. From the great hall drifted the sounds of music and the clatter of crockery as servant-girls set places for the feast.

The impression was one of normality. Every night Don Julius's men guarded the outer walls while the courtiers indulged themselves at table with music, fine food and bright conversation. To Don Julius and his minions, locked in their cocoon of pleasure and denial of reality, it would almost seem that tonight was no different from any other.

Which was exactly how Morgan and Ken Waldo wanted it to seem — just like any other night. If Morgan genuinely expected to reach the inner sanctum of Colonel Moro tonight then he must at least ensure that the enemy soldiers were off guard and not sharply watchful.

Even so, Morgan suspected that the odds against his surviving a mission which even his men insisted was loco, had to be slim bordering on the non-existent.

'Pow!' whispered Waldo, pointing his shooter at an imaginary adversary. 'Pow! Pow! Pow! Four shots, four clean hits on Mr Moro. All in the head. The greaser colonel's brain is splattered all over the goddamn joint, his guards panic and are runnin' round like headless chickens and you and yours truly are off over the wall in our hotsy-totsy Mex suits and snaking away along the riverbank headed for home afore they can figger for sure if Moro was jumped by men or will o' the wisps. Waddaya say, big man?'

'I say,' Morgan responded, almost wearily, 'that there are times when you remind me too much of Flash Damaron, mister.

You both talk too much, think you're too wonderful to live and never know when to shut up or quit. Don't you see the resemblance, junior?'

Handsome and swaggering in trimmed Mexican velvet, outsized sombrero and rowel spurs, the bunch's youngest gun-hand shot his leader a sly sideways glance.

'I been called worse things than old Flash's soul brother, Morg. I mean, so he's a double-crossin' son of a bitch and deserves shooting. But the man is still chain-lightning fast and he's got guts to burn like he proved by coming after you the way he did. Right?'

Morgan didn't respond. He regretted saying anything. He checked out his Colts, a hard frown creasing his brow. He was edgy, he knew, which was why he'd taken a shot at the kid. He understood the reason for it. It wasn't what was awaiting him on the other side of the moat that was nagging at him. It was the other thing.

That factor was his sixth sense which was working overtime as frogs renewed their chorusing from the river and starlight cast soft shadows across the valley.

He couldn't pinpoint just what it was about this place that played on his nerves. It could be Iselda, the daughter or even gabby Waldo himself. He only knew that tonight there was the unmistakable stink of something not quite right about Hacienda St Leque, and his inability to identify it set his nerves on edge.

Was he making a big mistake? Two men against the whole damn valley? What sort of odds would Eddie the bookie give a man on surviving a caper like that back at the El Paradiso cantina in Taos Pueblo?

Write your own ticket, most likely. And still lose.

Ken Waldo crossed the flagstone floor of the armaments room where they were making their final preparations. Soon they would head down for the secret tunnel that would spit them out at the dock where a rowboat waited to ferry them across the moat. The darkness promised to be their friend both during that perilous short journey as well as the dangerous miles down to Ascension.

Waldo's outsized spurs jingled musically as he drew to a halt.

'Know how many times you've mentioned old Flash in my hearing in two days, Morg?'

Morgan glanced up in irritation. 'Meaning?'

'Could be it means you've still got that gunner on your mind more'n you might think.'

'You're out of your head, kid. You proved that by volunteering to come with me tonight.'

'Let's not change the subject, eh, boss? I'd just like to know why you go on brooding about that feller.'

'You are nuts.'

'Maybe not.' The gunboy was serious now. 'You see, we all of us know Flash and what the bastard's capable of. Occurs to me that the reason you got him on your mind might be you're figgering he just might give the greasers the slip, get back here and come after us tonight. You know? The last damned thing we'd need.'

Morgan actually grinned for the first time.

'Seems to me you're the one that's worrying, kid. Well, for the last time, I'm not worrying about Damaron, haven't given him a thought.'

The slick boy's smile flashed as he stepped back and spread his hands.

'In that case, that leaves only one other explanation for why you're actin' kinda different. You're either in love or you're getting old.'

That set Morgan thinking. Not about love, unfortunately; he understood the true reason why Iselda had brought him down here from Arizona now and it had almost nothing to do with love.

But getting old? That would explain a lot, he figured.

But he'd die before he'd admit it.

'I'll never be as old as you, mister.

Know why? You play with death and that makes you older than any eighty-years-old geezer on his last legs and a country mile older than me, pilgrim.'

The kid looked impressed. 'If you say so, Morg.'

'What I say is let's cut the jaw and get on with the job!'

★   ★   ★

The tightly folded slip of paper weighted by a pebble glided down from one of the hacienda's windows, to be eventually captured by a shadowy figure by the wall. It was instantly flung across the oily waters of the moat where another figure appeared to snatch it up before vanishing in the direction of the distant town.

'There!' breathed Lucetta Diaz. 'It is done.'

Chavez hugged her. The couple stood together gazing off at the sprinkle of lights across the valley floor. It was still fifteen minutes before Morgan was scheduled to quit the hacienda, sufficient time for their message to reach the stone bunker headquarters of Colonel Moro and for him to dispatch troopers to Second Fording, where Morgan proposed crossing the river.

'Excellent, *chiquita*,' purred Chavez in a silky voice. 'You have just passed your greatest test of loyalty to the cause.'

'Have I, *hombrecito*? Have I really?'

'*Sí*, of course. When you were able to persuade your father to inform you of Morgan's secret plan to kill Moro tonight, you showed me beyond all doubt that you are committed to our cause to set the valley free.'

'It still seems strange to me that we must assist the colonel in order to benefit the poor, though, Johnny.'

'Not strange, Lucetta. Sensible. For should the mercenaries continue as they have done up until now, why, they might eventually get to defeat Moro and drive him from the valley altogether. Should that happen then your father would again reclaim his former power as ruler of Moritomo, and you know what that would mean, do you not?'

'That the peons would never be set free?'

'*Sí*. One despot is as bad as another. There is no difference between Moro's rule and the don's. Therefore we must assist Moro to defeat your father and pray that this victory shall cost him dearly, weaken him. Only then shall I be able to lead the rebel poor against the regiment. And this time they shall be successful. For the first time for almost one hundred years, Moritomo will be controlled by those to whom it rightly belongs, the oppressed and the enslaved themselves.'

'Oh, Johnny, you are so fine, so good.' The girl straightened and set her small, firm jaw. She nodded. '*Sí*, I am now proud I have sent Morgan to his certain death at the fording.'

'That is my loved one!'

'And if needs be, that my parents

should also die.'

'It may well come to that, little one.'

'And they will have none to blame but themselves, my love.'

The expression of admiration which crossed the smooth features of Johnny Chavez at that moment was totally genuine.

And yet he wondered again whether Lucetta Diaz might have inherited some of the madness afflicting her doting mother.

For Lucetta was doing the sort of things now that even he might balk at. She had embraced both himself and the 'cause' with a conviction that was absolute. At times he felt almost a little frightened himself by her ruthlessness and single-mindedness.

Chavez had been quick to recognize that these qualities in the girl he professed to love could prove of great assistance to him in his role as undercover agent for Colonel Moro. And he had certainly enjoyed the dalliance, while it lasted.

But of course no man could trust a woman with so much of the tiger in her make-up, he told himself sensibly. Once he had completed his rise to power and either shared or held alone complete control of the valley, he would have to bid *adios* to dark-eyed, cold-blooded Lucetta Diaz. With a bullet.

★ ★ ★

Flash Damaron slowly opened his eyes. For a long moment he was unaware of where he was or what that stink was, and howcome everything in that short space of time seemed so quiet.

Then he groaned and sat up straighter on his plank bench and felt the pain in his back where the whip had slashed the flesh.

In that instant reality came rushing back over him and his bruised and swollen lips silently framed the words 'Rio Toro!' And he cursed.

'You OK, Flash?'

Wilson's familiar voice seemed to

echo in the cage of the gunfighter's skull until it was drowned out by a sudden roar of brutal sound from somewhere outside which seemed to make the whole building vibrate.

It was the second time that day that the new prisoners had heard a ragged volley of gunfire erupt from the prison yard. The crash of the guns overpowered the dull sound of roped and bleeding bodies striking the hard surface of the execution yard, the sounds continuing to echo between the walls of the jail and the ruins of the mission of the Golden Virgin next door.

'Us next?' Wilson's voice was one rub above a whisper.

'Who cares?'

But Damaron cared. The gunman was not afraid of dying, only of not living long enough to exact his revenge on the man who had put him here. While ever Morgan lived and he himself breathed, he would go on hating and plotting his escape.

Forty-eight hours in a jolting, unsprung

prison wagon had carried the pair a long way southwest of Moritomo Valley to the grotesquely ugly town of Rio Toro, famed — or notorious — only for its prison, the men who died there and those who prayed for death every day.

The *Yanqui* gunmen had received the standard Rio Toro welcome, starvation, whippings, vilification and sleep deprivation. Tough Parlee Wilson had cracked and started in blubbering once or twice but their jailers had drawn nothing but stoic defiance or the occasional curse from Flash Damaron. Even if the gunman secretly believed he might well languish here until he simply rotted away, he gave no sign that he ever permitted that possibility to occupy his mind.

Instead he focused on the glory days when he had walked the big streets of Dodge City and Taos like a king. When he tired of summoning these visions from the past he could concentrate on revenge.

He would not spare any of those

who'd played even the most casual role in his fall. But of course the first and fiercest of his paybacks would be focused on Morgan.

He cursed at the thought and shook his head. The flies were back. For a short time they had deserted the cells to fly out to the heat-stricken execution yard and the sagging, bullet-riddled dead whose fresh blood was soaking into chinks between the paving stones there.

Now the flies were returning, sluggish and satiated, to buzz slowly around the cells and await the cool of the evening when they would at last settle on the oozing walls for their night's repose.

The new prisoners had been sadistically informed by their jailers that far more men went completely crazy in Rio Toro than were ever executed or died from natural causes.

Damaron knew he could die here. But it would never be from weakness, fear or despair. There was steel in his make-up, always had been. Apart from that, hate would keep him alive, that and the dream of vengeance. First Morgan, then Moro followed by whatever was left of the gunfighter bunch ... Don Julius, everyone who had taken part in his capture and transportation to the grisliest hell-hole in the province.

It was a good dream and he would never relinquish it if he rotted here twenty years. It was all he had, but it was enough.

★   ★   ★

Leading the way along the rocky river bank through the trees, Morgan felt the way he liked to be — quick, powerful and tinglingly alert in every fiber.

Getting old?

The hell he was!

'Morg!'

The whisper came from the slim shadow walking at his heels.

'What now? I told you no more talk, kid!'

'Boss man, I reckon I've got your problem now. Must be catchin'.'

Morgan stopped in his tracks.

'What?'

The river rushed through this patch of woods, all but drowning their voices. A half-mile farther along, the Rio Abreau, after winding its white-water way out of the Toro Sierras, rushed headlong downslope for a mile or two before reaching the valley floor, where it assumed a more leisurely pace on its meandering journey down the eastern flank of the valley.

Here sturdy trees grew between slabs of rock and the river-fed grasses grew thickly. A boulder they passed bore a fading crust-colored smear where a trooper had fallen to his death in a gun battle several days earlier. Timber blocked off sight of both town and hacienda from here, feeble starlight struggled hard to penetrate the foliage overhead.

Nature protected the intruder here but beyond the fording the valley farmlands and pastures opened up and there would be far less cover for two night-walkers intent on mischief.

Just what shape that mischief might take was something Morgan would decide after assessing the danger level at the crossing. He wanted to strike the enemy a major blow, would walk over hot coals for a chance to get one clear shot at Moro himself. Failing that, whatever moral or actual damage they might be able to cause by a lightning raid might be enough to swing the pendulum of this conflict their way.

'You know how you was feelin' jittery earlier on, Morg?' panted the slim-hipped gunslick from Blue Sky Mesa. 'Well, now you're cool as settin' butter but I'm gettin' twitchy. Don't that beat all?'

'Judas Priest! You bore the world about how feisty you are, now you start coming apart just when I make up my mind to count on you!'

'Don't get me wrong. Sure, I am jittery now — can't deny it. But that always makes me twice as fast. But, damnit man, of a sudden I got me this here feelin'.'

'What feeling?' Morgan wanted to keep moving, but he'd never seen Ken Waldo show unease.

He saw the whites of the gunfighter's eyes flicker in the leafy gloom. 'Why . . . like I ain't gonna make it, mebbe.'

'That tears it! Get your sorry ass back to the hacienda and — '

'No, Morg, you're readin' me wrong. I'm ready to lick my weight in wildcats and . . . ' His voice faded away for a moment. 'It's just that if I was to die then I wouldn't be leavin' much behind, would I?'

Morgan might have snapped at the youth again but he didn't. For, unawares, Ken Waldo had put into words exactly what he himself had been feeling. For what did a mercenary ever leave behind him but a string of graves and, if he was lucky, a few weeping women?

'Come on, kid.' His tone was almost

gentle. 'You can search your goddamn soul all you please when we get back to the hacienda.'

'What'll you leave behind, big man?'

'You're testing my patience, Waldo!'

'You're different from the rest of us, boss.' The gunboy spoke with quick urgency now. 'Some of the boys reckon you're immortal, and they could be right. But you've already done your share and made your mark. This'll likely be the last really big job you'll ever take on. All we want to leave, when our time comes, is a good woman and someplace to call home where a man might raise some kids and chickens before the big dark comes down — '

He rested his hand on Morgan's arm. 'But take the word of a man who's older than he looks, old son. You ain't never gonna find what you're searchin' for down here in Mexico. And never with the don's wife. She's — '

'OK, you just used up your last gab ticket,' Morgan rapped. 'I'm going on. You can come with me, go back to St

Leque, or stay here all night spouting buffalo dust until one of Moro's men happens along and puts a bullet through your head. I'm gone!'

Before the boy could object he was off at the run. Waldo stared after him a moment, then smartly followed.

The timber thinned as they neared Second Fording. They knew the crossing here was often undermanned. Morgan slowed his steps when he glimpsed the white road leading down to the water. The fording was flanked by ancient boulders which appeared blue and ghostly in the starlight. Before Morgan realized what the other had in mind, Waldo was darting past him, twin gunbarrels glinting in his hands.

'Let's see who's got the grit in his gizzard now, old man,' he taunted. 'Last one across sucks eggs!'

Reaching the edge of the rushing water, Waldo stopped sharply, swung his head and grinned at the older man, cocky, full of life and afraid of nothing.

As always. Their eyes met for a moment and Morgan felt something like a smile cross his face.

The flat whiplike crack of a rifle sounded above the rushing of the river. Shot through the head, Waldo gasped and tumbled backwards into the water, to vanish instantly from sight.

The fording erupted with a volley of guns and tongues of gunflame came searching for Morgan where he crouched amongst the giant boulders.

Ambush!

Morgan hit dirt and fanned his gun hammer to loose a scythe of shots at the shadowy figures suddenly coming visible along the stony riverbank. A man screamed in total agony and was driven back into another by a .45 slug. Both tumbled into the torrent to be instantly swept away.

A slug whipped so close to Morgan's face that he felt the heat of it passing.

He dived headlong in search of better cover, then swept up his sixgun to take aim again. Another trooper went down, clutching at his throat and vomiting blood.

Morgan jumped erect. Two figures came rushing from the trees. Dropping to a low crouch, he fanned his Colt's hammer and chopped them down. They fell like wheatsheaves, rustling, lifeless.

He leapt over the bodies and burst from cover, fanning the hammer of his second sixgun, pouring a hail of bullets into the ghostly outlines of the enemy. He was once again what he had been all his life. A killing machine. Times like this he could figure what people were going to do before they did it. Could hit any target without taking aim. He could feel the grisly breath of Old Man Death on his neck and didn't give a damn. Times like this Clay Morgan almost believed what some said about him. That he was immortal.

Second Fording was still dangerous territory but the enemy ranks were thinning, some dead, others now running like yellow dogs.

Suddenly he was up, then down, now zigzagging through the timber before abruptly doubling back after fully reloading to blast three blood-pumping figures backwards into the river, their weapons flying high and one man begging God to forgive him his sins even as he sank beneath the waters, while another cursed the same Creator with his dying breath.

Next instant Morgan was plunging headlong after the swirling corpses. He kicked deep below the surface, the sound of enemy fire making harmless-seeming plip-plop noises above his head. He moved swiftly downstream, carried by the current and boosted by his own powerful overhand stroking.

When eventually he was forced to surface, lungs bursting, he found himself a far piece below the fording. He quit the river at the first stand of riverside timber and headed directly for the distant town.

The best place for a man to hide himself was in a crowd. And that was the only option he had left now, he realized. His reckless plan had been to bust out of the hacienda, then rely upon pumped-up nerve, a fast gun and fool's luck to get him to Moro and blow him out of his fancy cowhide boots. No hope of that now. He'd tried and failed. All that remained now was the slender hope of saving his own neck.

He threw a glance over his shoulder as powerful legs carried him into a head-high field of corn. 'Adios, kid,' he muttered aloud. 'You died game.'

He wasn't even aware he said it.

★   ★   ★

They were closing in.

Moro had every available man assigned to the manhunt now and the fugitive mercenary had about run out of places to hide.

Pounding down a narrow back-street of the jittery town flanked by the whitewashed adobes of the poor, Morgan skidded on something wet and gluggy, and crashed shoulder-first into a porch awning which collapsed with a crash. He whipped around the next corner and came face to face with two startled figures in military gray toting long rifles and each boasting handlebar moustaches.

'Ees heem?' gasped the big one.

Morgan didn't give them time to find out who he might be. He simply cut loose with twin Colts and kept blasting until he had the smoke-filled street all to himself.

A doorway loomed ahead. Morgan was making for it when more soldiers appeared dimly at the mouth of the street 200 feet distant.

Suddenly the door swung open. Before he could trigger; a strong hand seized him by the shirtfront and hauled him into the darkness.

'What in hell — ?'

'Quiet or you will kill us all!' a stern voice commanded.

It was a woman's voice.

★ ★ ★

Black-winged, yellow-beaked and sinister, the great Sonoran buzzard glided across the cornfields and then spread its pinions to land with a curious grace upon the crossbeam from which two corpses hung suspended.

The smaller of the two corpses was undeniably that of Ken Waldo, slick, cocky and gunfast no longer. His companion in death was a tall, heavy-shouldered figure attired in the the same sort of clothing that Clay Morgan was wearing the night before when he had quit Hacienda St Leque on his ill-fated mission to assassinate Colonel Moro.

A second buzzard came to perch upon the crossbeam and yet another two appeared in the distance winging in from the east. The timber cross with its grim hanging trophies had been erected within a Winchester shot of the hacienda's northern walls during the hours of darkness.

Dawn's light found the parapets of the besieged fortress lined with sober, silent faces. Some wept, some cursed as the two buzzards dropped lower, perched upon Waldo's shoulder, then ripped at the white face with cruel talons. Crazy Jake blasted off three angry shots but the devil birds ignored them.

Standing apart from the others, Buck Clooney shook his head and repeated over and over like a litany: 'It ain't Morg. I just know it ain't him.'

'Mebbe, mebbe not,' muttered a haggard Gunner Jills. 'But ain't no doubt that's young Kenny by his side ... ' The hardcase paused a moment then began to sing:

> It was on one dark night
> That young Waldo died
> When he and Clay Morgan
> They ventured outside —

'Can that!' snapped Crazy Jake and glanced away at the parapet where the don and his lady were to be seen staring off fixedly at the grisly figures on the gaunt frame far below.

Don Julius then turned to stare across at his lady in silence. For the first time there was hopelessness in the aristo's expression. His wife didn't see it. She barely saw the swinging corpses. But she believed one of those corpses to be Morgan and already her troubled mind was laboriously at work searching for some way in which she might yet continue to save her daughter from the fate that appeared to be closing in on them all. The doña wept, but her tears were not for Clay Morgan. They were all shed for her only love, her princess.

★　★　★

Soledad Engracia said, 'Cornbread?'

Morgan replied, 'I can eat cornbread until the world looks level.'

'Chilli?'

'Why not?'

It wasn't Morgan's customary authoritative tone. He sounded almost flippant. Likely he was a little light-headed from the combination of regret and relief, fatigued from being hounded, dogged and shot at by a small army of provincial troopers, wonder at finding himself still alive in the first hour of daylight as Moro's search for the 'big gringo' moved away to other parts of Ascension.

The woman gazed down at him pensively as he attacked the chillies and cornbread like a condemned man consuming his last meal.

She was tall, full-figured and earthy in the way some peasant women are. She'd told him she lived here alone with two small children, now sleeping. Her husband had left her, to join up and die with a rebel army in the sierras the previous year. She had also confided that she despised Moro, hated the Diazes, made a living as a seamstress and hoped one day to live on the land and raise corn.

Morgan had not been obliged to tell Soledad Engracia about himself. She already knew. Mere weeks earlier, few here had ever even heard of a gringo

149

soldier of fortune named Clay Morgan. Now every peasant in the valley knew exactly who and what he was; every man, woman and child appeared to be confused as to whether they should curse the very name of Clay Morgan as a hired pistoleer of the detested Don Julius or laud him as a genuine hero for overcrowding their local cemetery with Colonel Moro's dead.

When the woman confided this to him Morgan just grunted and went on eating. He was still marveling at the wonder of being alive when by rights he should be a dozen times dead.

7

DEAD MAN WALKING

'More son-a-beech soup, *hombre*?'

Morgan dabbed at his mouth with his bandanna. 'Not right now.' He studied her frankly. 'You're a good cook.'

She shrugged as she gathered up the plates. 'I should not waste good food on such as you.'

'Huh?'

'Moro, the son of a diseased dog, will find you and hang you.' Another shrug. 'Wasted.'

Morgan grinned and searched his pockets in vain for tobacco. As though anticipating him, Soledad produced tin, cigarette papers and lucifers. She watched him as he deftly rolled a smoke and set it alight.

'Sit down and tell me some more about everyone down here.'

'Everyone?'

'Moro, the Diazes, how it all began . . . you know?'

The Mexican woman appeared totally at ease now as she took a chair on the other side of the table and began to speak in a soft yet strong voice, about how the valley had, following centuries of oppression by *bandidos*, demagogues and plundering hordes from the south, eventually come to be dominated by the Diaz family, who took over with such ruthless efficiency and brutality that the peon and the poor saw little difference between one exploiting tyrant and another.

Yet the poor still dreamed of peace and when Colonel Moro rose to power in the province they sought his patronage, which he gave willingly with bullet, bayonet, prison, taxes, until it came down to what now might be seen as the final titanic struggle to see which demagogue would rule Moritomo Valley.

Morgan nodded with cynical amusement. The stories were always the same down here. They must know what their future must always be, he mused, and yet this handsome woman before him seemed to him to possess something extra, some deep quality of strength and self-assurance which appeared to enable her to lift herself above the morass of reality she lived in, giving her rare dignity and presence.

The peons still dreamed of owning and working their own land despite the current chaos, she went on. That was their only dream. And Morgan saw it as that and nothing more. The impossible dream. At least that was surely the case here in sunny Mexico. In the States, he'd made a healthy if dangerous living helping men fight for land rights, both genuine and fraudulent. There was corruption in government in Arizona and Texas but it was not endemic as it was south of the border.

He reckoned he could help these folk, but they could never afford him.

Besides, they had troubles enough. Mostly when he enforced 'peace and justice' anyplace, the big winners were the undertakers.

He frowned and stared down at the hard-packed earth of the peasant woman's walled yard. That might well be an honest assessment of the Morgan profession, but it didn't make it sound any better to his own ears right at that moment.

He supposed, thoughtfully munching chillies between powerful teeth, that deep down he was a peon himself. At least it was true that the only genuine lifetime ambition he'd ever had was one day to own his own private piece of dirt, hang up the Colts, get fat and only ever look at the newspapers to check on stock-prices.

'Why?' he demanded after a silence, mopping up chilli sauce with a stub of cornbread.

'Why . . . ?'

'Why'd you haul me in here like you did, *señora*? They'll slick your throat and likely your babies too if they find out what you did.'

For a time she didn't answer. She sat in profile across the table and he studied her with a deepening interest that puzzled him. There was something about Mexican women, he reflected. They seemed to have more of everything that was feminine and desirable in womankind than their sisters north of the border. Soledad Engracia wasn't beautiful but was generously proportioned, totally feminine and possessed a kind of challenging poise and quick intelligence which he found oddly alluring.

For a moment Iselda flicked into his mind then was gone. 'Well, lady?' he challenged.

'I did what I did for two reasons,' she replied, pouring him more coffee. 'The first is because my father, Miguel, is a leader of people's rights against all our many oppressors. I despise Diaz, but Moro would be an even greater tyrant . . . and you, *hombre*, are one of the greatest threats to the colonel's ambitions . . . '

'Uh huh. So that's one.'

'The other is . . . ' She paused, then went on: 'When I saw you run by earlier, I thought, 'Soledad, that must be the first man who really looks like a man since your beloved Paolo died . . . '

Morgan leaned back in his chair. He was full, relaxed and growing drowsy. That was no way for a man on the run to feel. He knew there was no guarantee he might survive the next half-hour, let alone the days ahead. He'd failed in his mission to put Moro in his grave, had seen Waldo die before his eyes. Knew he should feel grim and grave even if he had cost the enemy dear . . . yet instead he was feeling oddly at peace here in this quiet yard with this woman and her food, her searching gaze and marvellous breasts . . .

'What are you saying?' he asked bluntly.

Instead of replying she rose gracefully

and led him indoors to her bedroom. She didn't have to beckon him twice.

★ ★ ★

Watching the distant hacienda from his bougainvillea-shrouded bunker along the river, the colonel now believed he could actually feel the defenders' deepening despair.

He smiled.

He was proud of his durability, inventiveness and enterprise and in particular of the way in which he had turned partial failure into a kind of victory.

For the idea to raid the mortuary in search of a Morgan-sized corpse from the many there awaiting burial had been his entirely. Some of his men had seen enough of the mercenary to ensure that the body was attired virtually identically to the missing gringo leader before it was hoisted high to swing in the gentle breeze alongside the authentic remains of Ken Waldo.

Despite his satisfaction with this ploy Moro still had a sizeable squad of men scouring the village inch by inch for the big gringo. Morgan was still very much alive so far as the colonel knew, and he wouldn't rest until that situation was altered.

He gazed about uneasily. He'd doubled his personal bodyguard and the streets and alleys nearby were well-policed by riflemen. Heads would roll if the mercenary wasn't caught.

In the meantime Colonel Moro must decide whether or not he should launch another full-scale attack before the don recovered from the perceived loss of the most powerful card in his deck.

* * *

Morgan watched the woman work.

He got the impression that Soledad Engracia made a reasonable living at her seamstress trade. She had lost her best clients after the blockading of the Hacienda St Leque and now Colonel

Moro provided most of her business. Moro had acquired many mistresses during his time in the valley and instead of paying them in cash for their favors he thought it more romantic to give them presents of blouses, skirts and embossed shawls, hence a great deal of business for Ascension's seamstress.

Pablo, the toddler, approached Morgan from across the sun-filled courtyard which was shielded by solid high fences. Unthinkingly, Morgan hefted the child to his knee and winked. Pablo stared up at him solemnly. The woman turned from her work, her face betraying momentary astonishment before she smiled.

'He likes you, *hombre*.'

'Could be.'

Morgan was in a strange frame of mind today. Last night he'd eluded death a dozen hair-raising times as what had seemed to him like the entire Moro regiment hounded him through the rabbit-warren of streets and alleys. In the process he had slain more men, two with the Colts and at least three with his Bowie. Today they'd redoubled their efforts. At that moment he could hear them pounding the pathways, still hunting for the big gringo.

While he sat in a courtyard soaking up the sun and dandling a baby on his knee.

How unlike Clay Morgan could this be?

Normally this sort of situation would galvanize him into action. Escape, tactics, survival — that would be all he'd have time for. Instead he felt this unaccountable languor creeping over him as he sipped bitter black coffee from a small earthenware mug and idly fingered a fresh bullet crease in his forearm which provided mute testimony to just how close he'd stepped to eternity the night before.

He wondered what was happening to him. Really.

At first he attributed his strange mood to a natural reaction to failure. Sure, he'd thinned the ranks of the enemy out at Second Fording, but that was not what he'd set out to do. His self-appointed task was to kill Moro and cause the siege to be lifted, when almost all he'd succeeded in doing was getting Waldo killed and coming within a whisker of losing his own life.

He sighed.

Now he was cut off from the hacienda, didn't fancy his chances of getting back there in one piece, and could not be sure just how long the others might survive up there without him around to tell them what to do and lead by murderous example.

He nodded and thought: he certainly had every good reason for feeling low.

But he didn't.

What he did feel was almost good, which had to be bad. A normal man who'd just taken a bad licking shouldn't feel anything but low. But his profession was different; he was different. Any man of the guns who walked as tall as did Clay Morgan had to win every time out, on account of winning was all you had.

Again his gaze was drawn to Soledad. Remembering last night he found himself uncharacteristically wondering if . . . no, it couldn't be. She was just another woman, nothing unique.

Wasn't she?

Momentarily his thoughts flickered to Iselda and a frown cut his dark brows. Poor Iselda. That was how he thought of her now; there was no other way to think. He was afraid people might be right . . . the things they said about her . . .

His gaze turned distant, his thoughts ranging back to other times. He was back in Blue Sky Mesa and Flash Damaron was attempting to goad him by alleging that Iselda Diaz might be less than normal.

Bastard!

Anyway, he'd paid that fast gun out for running off at the mouth. But that didn't alter hard-edged reality. The way Iselda had spoken that night they made love at the hacienda, painting a verbal picture of a sick and diseased world in which her daughter was the only possible thing worth protecting or worth fighting for, had made him realize her tortured state of mind.

He was not so shocked that he could not see the irony of it all, however; the gunfighter who'd struggled to fall in love as a way of redemption had unwittingly chosen someone as warped by life as himself.

Morgan was sick. He'd realized it for some time now. Sick of the life, the slaughter, the sheer brutal aimlessness of it all. His searching for love, he sensed, was like a physically ill man struggling to find a cure for what ailed him.

He knew of a small town in Arizona not far from Fortune City on the fringe of the desert where lungers came to escape the colder climes. He'd seen them there, shuffling and coughing in the hot, dry air. His lungs were fine. It was his heart that was sick.

'Wipe his nose.'

Morgan emerged from his reverie at

the sound of Soledad's voice. 'Huh?'

She indicated the child. Morgan caught on. He used his Mexican bandanna to clean the child's nose. Pablo got down and toddled away to play with his sister. The boy was two, Maria four. Their father had died young and violently but Soledad did not appear bitter or self-pitying. Instead she radiated a kind of earthy strength which he had witnessed often in Mexican women, yet rarely in females of his own race.

'You see?' she smiled with just a hint of irony. 'Every day a person can learn something new, no?'

Morgan tugged out his cigar-case. Still decked out in his Mexican disguise, he sat with his shirt unbuttoned halfway to the waist, soaking up the sun. He was hatless and his skin gleamed like oiled bronze. It was mighty odd, he mused. At that very moment, and despite the fact that he could hear the voices of troopers loudly questioning someone about him further along the street, he felt strangely secure and at peace, almost as though he belonged here in this alien land, oblivious of any danger. He felt content. All he could think about was what they would eat.

Maybe this was what men meant when they talked about 'goin' Mex.' He studied Soledad.

She was larger and lighter-skinned than most Mexican women — not fat, simply built on a more generous scale. The tint of her skin was almost golden and it looked well with her brown eyes and black hair. She went barefoot about her adobe and her attire was a roomy white shirt and comfortable peasant skirt.

As she bent in concentration to snip off a stitch, tiny beads of perspiration glinted between her deep breasts and her bent arm showed the smooth bulge of strength.

'What are you looking at?' she asked without glancing up.

'Is there a law against looking here?'

'Law? What is that?'

'It sure ain't what you folks live under down here.'

He got to his feet and stretched heavy arms. 'Don't you ever get to thinking about fighting for your rights instead of just sitting back and letting anyone who happens by ride roughshod right over you?'

'When you fight you die.'

'Wrong. I've been fighting all my life. I'm still here.'

'You are not like other men.'

'It ain't how big and cussed you are so much as what's in here.' He struck his chest. 'I've never seen country as rich and pretty as this, yet all you people live pretty much in slavery. First you let the don run your lives, now Moro. I don't get it.'

'Are you trying to say you like it here?'

'Yeah . . . mebbe.'

'Would a man like you help us fight?'

Morgan was peeved by her question. Seemed the only real interest anyone ever showed in him was related to his gun prowess. Didn't he have any quality or attraction apart from that?

Without responding he went to the bench where he'd left his Colts. He began cleaning them, aware of the woman watching from the corner of her eye. Suddenly the adobe vibrated to the sound of heavy knocking at the door giving on to the alley. Morgan snatched up his Colts but Soledad, quickly to her feet, waved him back, placed a silencing finger to her lips and vanished inside.

It proved to be an interesting conversation that Morgan overheard as he stood by the door, ready to blast anybody and everybody who might come through it.

'Ahh, the brave soldiers!' Soledad's tone was laced with irony. 'It is not enough to keep me awake half the night with your shooting and shouting, now you will ruin my day also.'

A man's voice answered.

'We must search the house, Soledad. This *pistolero* is still at large.'

'My babies are asleep and I am working. Tell the colonel I will not have his work finished by tomorrow if I am to be interrupted.'

'But, Soledad — '

'Shoo! Vamoose! What is it? Do you think I hide a *fugitivo* beneath my skirts? But wait. You poor *hombres* look half-starved from all your chasing and not finding anything. *Un momento* and I will bring you some cakes.'

Morgan heard the slap of her bare feet, the uncertain muttering of the men at the door. His guns were both on full cock. Should they force their way in he would slaughter them both without a moment's hesitation. He glanced at the children and bit his lip. Gunfighting around kids now, Morgan? It doesn't get any better, does it.

It didn't come to that. The searchers got their cakes, jocularly accused Soledad of being too big and bossy for her own good, but left with no concern that the colonel's seamstress might be hiding a fugitive, for which the penalty in Moritomo Valley was death.

The woman did not reappear for some time. When she did, she brought fresh cake and a platter of fragrant sultana cakes.

She couldn't understand Morgan's silence as they formed an idyllic picture of peace and tranquility seated together at the garden table with the children playing around their feet.

In the lazy sun-soaked silence, Morgan the mercenary wondered whether he mightn't be going a little loco. Here he was with just an adobe wall between him and God knew how many hairy-faced greasers with big guns hunting for him, and all he could think about was whether he should limit himself to two cakes or go for broke and polish off a third.

Soledad had no way of understanding how peaceful and contented he was feeling at that moment.

But the clocks kept ticking and soon duty was calling him with an ever increasingly shrill voice. His reckless

plan to quit the hacienda and take
Moro out of the equation via the sixgun
solution, had proved a failure and an
almost total disaster. But that was
yesterday's news. Deep down, he
sensed he was ready to quit both his
contract and Mexico right now. He
could, quite easily. But of course he
would not.

Everything he was, every tenet he
lived by dictated that he must return to
Hacienda St Leque. He would wait
until full dark. And he wanted to wait.
With this woman here in this calm,
peaceful place.

'You do not eat your cake, *hombre*.'

'Don't nag me, lady.'

'Eat!'

Momentarily Morgan's gray eyes
flared cold. Then the little girl tugged at
his pants leg. He bent and gave her a
bite of his cake. He looked up and met
Soledad's imperious eye. Then he
obediently lifted the cake to his lips and
took a bite. She smiled warmly and
began to hum some soft Andalusian

melody. The sun was warm and good on Morgan's back. He wondered if he would survive the next twenty-four hours.

★　★　★

With every passing hour their mood grew darker. Several of the mercenaries believed the corpse they had watched being torn to pieces by the buzzard to be that of Morgan. Others insisted he was still alive. The proof, they argued, was the uniformed troopers whom they could still see combing both valley and town as the long afternoon wore on.

They believed they were still hunting Morgan down there and that Moro had hung up someone else roughly Morgan's size alongside Waldo to shatter their morale.

If that were the case, the colonel's ploy appeared to be succeeding.

A massive pall of gloom had settled all across the besieged stronghold as the grim day progressed. And now, without

Morgan himself at the helm, the gunfighters were little different from the others. They swaggered, they smoked incessantly, they talked tough. But they were not doing anything. This train was running without a locomotive and slowing towards a dead halt.

'Capons!' the don said caustically, watching from an alcove surrounded by his retainers as Clooney and Kit Chiller passed by. 'Where is their spirit, their pride?'

'Such brave words,' his daughter said to her young man, seated some distance from the main group. 'You will of course note that my father is himself . . . so brave, standing bare-chested at the barricades defying the foe to do their worst! Such a hypocrite!'

Chavez studied her curiously.

'Why do you hate your father so, Lucetta?'

'I do not hate him. I merely hold him in contempt.'

'And your mother?'

'There is, as you may know, a

hospital in Los Lunas where they care for the weak of mind. It is where my mother will go when the revolution is successful and the poor rule the land again as they once did before my grandfather's coming. Does that answer your question?'

'Yet she loves you so,' he said wonderingly. 'I have never known a mother more devoted to a daughter.'

'She smothers me with her love,' she replied bitterly. 'Besides, for years she has supported the don in his cruelty and exploitation of the peons. She is as guilty as he is.'

The young man ran fingers through his glossy black curls. '*Chiquita*, is it possible that when we met and I told you I was involved in helping the peons overthrow their rulers, that you at last found a reason to justify your hatred of your parents, where before you had none? Is that why you have taken up the cause with such fervor?'

It was a cruel question. But it did not throw Lucetta Diaz for a moment. With a toss of her hair, she snapped, 'It is merely a convention to love one's parents or they you. I broke that convention long before you came into my life, Johnny Chavez.'

He nodded. He considered himself lucky to have met Lucetta when he had. Sent into the hacienda as a spy by Colonel Moro, Chavez had needed an influential contact in the don's fortress and had secured it with the girl. He had sensed both her vicious nature and her hostility towards her parents from the outset, and had used both to his advantage. Lucetta lived to hate, and Chavez encouraged her in this. Her assistance would be crucial to him as events moved towards their inevitable climax.

Chavez turned his gaze to the valley. Dust rose sluggishly above the distant adobes; men were on the move. Utilizing their secret signalling system, the colonel had informed his spy that he intended to take full advantage of the blow to St Leque morale that had resulted from the deaths of Waldo and Morgan. Tonight he would launch his most intense, and, he hoped, final assault.

And Chavez would play an essential role in that attack. He was going to lower the drawbridge. He knew he couldn't do it alone; the bridgehouse was the most heavily guarded sector in the entire fortress. It was off limits to virtually everyone but its security and operators. Yet Lucetta the princess was free to go there wherever she chose. And Chavez was certain she would do whatever he asked in order to see her father vanquished by Colonel Moro. She was that sick.

He'd convinced his willing young disciple that there was in existence a powerful and committed force of ragged rebels waiting to unleash itself as soon as Moro and her father had weakened one another sufficiently to open the door to the grand revolution.

There was, of course, no rebel army. It was pure fiction. But at least it existed in the girl's mind and that in itself would prove sufficient to enable him to get her to do anything he wanted when the final hour struck.

When the drawbridge came down tonight, Moro would lead his assembled troops headlong into the hacienda to destroy the weary Don Julius, his demoralized *ricos* and the handful of Arizonan mercenaries who would be trying to fight without their dynamic leader.

Lovely Lucetta would be waiting for her romantic rebel army to arise and swarm over both victor and vanquished when the bloody battle was decided, but it would never happen.

Yet tonight would certainly mean the end of her father, as Chavez had promised. However, it would not mark the opening of any peon revolution, only the triumph of the colonel, and one of his most effective undercover men.

And triumph would be certain, so Chavez assured himself, because the

Diaz family was so fatally flawed. The father was a victim of blind arrogance, the mother was sliding into insanity, the doted-upon daughter was filled with selfish, unreasoning hatred fuelled by bogus idealism.

Johnny Chavez took Lucetta's hand and kissed it gallantly. She smiled at him with her black eyes in a way that chilled him. She was truly dangerous, he realized, and he reaffirmed his earlier decision that the don's daughter could not be allowed to survive the night ahead.

For when she discovered how he had deceived and used her, all that twisted hatred would be unleashed upon him. He was too much of an *hombre* to concede that this prospect scared him. Yet it did.

★　★　★

At exactly 3 p.m. the colonel's repaired cannon announced the resumption of hostilities with the dinosaur bellow of its angry voice. The explosion of the shell against the hacienda's battered walls in turn ushered in the clatter of the Gatling and the spang and rattle of rifle fire from the enemy positions, once again fully manned by uniformed soldiers.

The defence was sporadic at best, and by five o'clock Buck Clooney was sniffing the air and reading the signs. He was grimacing and sniffing as he and Kit Chiller took turns at sniping at the enemy through a narrow rifle port in the west wall.

'What?' growled rugged Chiller, pausing to reload his carbine. 'You catchin' cold or somethin', old man?'

'Bein' funny don't suit you, Chiller.'

'You reckon sniffin' and scowlin' suits you?' Chiller took a second look at the veteran, sobered.

'What is it?'

'I can smell it, pard.'

'Smell what?'

'Defeat. It's in the air. Take a look around you. They figure Morg's gone and they're dyin' on their feet.'

Kit Chiller did as he was bid. He saw the don's men crouching in cover where they should be manning the walls. He glimpsed Wyatt and Dundee talking when they ought to be making preparations to repel the next assault. He sniffed and realized he could also detect the scent of defeat. It was stronger than the stink of gunsmoke.

'Well, leastways me and you ain't gonna hand it to 'em on a platter, old timer,' tough Chiller growled, stepping back. 'Your turn.'

Chiller still couldn't believe Morgan was dead. He'd figured he was immortal. They all had.

8

WHERE SIEGEMEN DIE

Soledad emitted a high laugh. 'No, Morgan! That is not how a woman walks. The hips, *hombre*, the hips!'

Morgan scowled. This had to be the lowest point in an illustrious career. He stood in the flower-patterned light of the adobe's parlor dressed in an ankle-length taffeta gown embroidered with red roses. He wore a black shoulder-length wig left behind by one of Soledad's customers, a becoming poke-bonnet and a stylish black mantilla that hung around his broad shoulders.

He studied his reflection critically in a full-length wall-mirror, trying to ignore the giggles of the woman in back of him. It was warm and comfortable in this snug house but even here you could still hear the snarling sounds of distant battle.

It was twenty-four hours since Morgan's 'death' at the hands of Moro's men and as a result the colonel was nearer final victory than ever before, so demoralizing had the apparent loss of their leader proved to be for the mercenary force at the hacienda. Things certainly looked bleak for the defenders up-valley, but Morgan was never the kind of man to give up without a fight. Soon — just as soon as he solved this problem with his hips — he would be back up there leading them just like always.

The woman had called his master plan suicidal but Morgan had no intention of dying. Which was the reason he was prepared to swallow his vanity and pride and accept a little expert advice about his hips and their rotation, or lack of it. His very survival might depend upon his getting it right when he was forced simply to saunter off through a town crawling with men with guns still searching for him.

'Don't just make a damn-fool state-ment then not follow it up, woman,' he growled. 'Exactly what ain't right about the hips, damnit?'

'They must roll,' she replied, giving him a sensual demonstration. 'Not like this.' Now she strode across the room mimicking Morgan's masculine gait. 'The first sentry you pass that way will take one look at the large *señorita* strutting through town and shout — 'it is him, the *fugitivo*!' — and begin the shooting.'

He nodded submissively and took a few tentative steps. The woman frowned, jabbed a finger at his hips and snapped, 'Roll! Roll! Roll!' After view-ing several more attempts by him to do just that, she tugged at her lower lip, shrugged and sighed.

'Well, as they will probably kill you no matter how well you walk I suppose it will do . . .'

Suddenly her playful manner van-ished and she was staring up at him with eloquent brown eyes in a way that made Morgan's throat tighten.

In truth there was much about himself and his feelings that puzzled him tonight. Never before had he experienced much trouble in simply walking away from anyone or anywhere. That had always been his way. He was a drifter moving constantly from one job to the next, never caring much where he wound up at the end of it providing he had money in his pocket and some kind of shelter over his head. But this was quite different, disturbingly so. Here in this little adobe home with this strong, gentle woman and her children, he experienced something he'd never known before — a feeling of peace. To leave that behind now and head out into that uncertain night and maybe never see her again . . .

'It is not too late to change your mind, *hombre*.'

Morgan cocked his head, as though he was listening to the gunfire. Yet his mind remained focused on himself and where he was. He stood rooted to the spot, seemingly unable to think what to do next, to decide. He was suddenly so angry with himself, with fate, with the whole damned iron inevitability of his life that at this moment he was incapable of doing anything other than moving slowly for the door.

Soledad beat him to it.

'You do not leave me without a goodbye — dead man!' she said passionately and when she hugged him to her then stood on tiptoe to crush her mouth against his, Morgan almost weakened.

Almost. Not quite. The habits of a lifetime were too deeply ingrained. Never quit on a job until it's finished. That was just one of the hard laws he'd lived by these twenty years and more and nothing was going to change it now.

For surely if ever a job cried out to be finished it was Hacienda St Leque.

He jerked the door open and stepped out into the narrow street. He didn't look back. Bending his knees to cut down his height and remembering to roll his hips while clutching a loaded and cocked sixshooter beneath his black lace shawl, he quickly put the street behind him and started boldly across the lamplit square.

Soledad had prayed to the Virgin of Guadaloupe for him that night and Morgan realized the saint must have been listening when he grew aware of a disturbance over by the gallows. Gray-garbed troopers were brawling with a bunch of peons, and he heard a brawny sergeant bellow: 'Throw them in irons, the rebellious scum. We shall deal with them tomorrow!'

What Morgan had no way of knowing was that a small miracle was taking place in Valley Moritomo that night. Although the 'rebel uprising' which Johnny Lopez had spoken of to Lucetta Diaz was purely imaginary, the real thing had erupted spontaneously amongst the peons at the end of a day that had seemed even uglier, more violent and intolerable to them than all the similar days they'd suffered through before.

The rumored death of Morgan the mercenary seemed to threaten their last hope of destroying Moro, and with a feeling of nothing left to lose one man had shot at a trooper, another had set fire to an official coach — and suddenly every undernourished and whip-scarred field worker was grabbing up a weapon — any weapon would do — and going after any man in army gray.

By the looks of things the pathetic rebellion was not having much success. Yet it wasn't without its merit insofar as it created a diversion which enabled a 240-pound *señorita* to make her hasty way across the dimly-lit square without attracting undue attention.

In the darkness of an alley, Morgan shed his disguise and went searching for a horse. He didn't find one but did manage to locate a bad-tempered jackass munching oaten hay in an unattended yard. Forking the ugly critter and using the head-stall to steer with, he trotted from the yard and headed south toward the sounds of the guns.

★   ★   ★

The vesta in Chavez's trembling fingers flared and set fire to the tinder which in turn lighted the kindling wood which then sent flames licking hungrily over the oil-soaked beams of the abandoned horse stables.

Moro's undercover man at the hacienda was shaking for good reason. If he was caught in this treachery it would mean certain execution.

He was sweating with relief by the time he returned to the lower court-yards unnoticed. Glancing back, he glimpsed a thin blue plume of smoke rising silently from the stable doors. Nodding in satisfaction, he clambered up the steep staircase which led past the post commanded by mercenaries Long-horn Bob and Gunner Jills. The two

Americans were trading desultory rifle fire with soldiers positioned out by the west trail. Some distance away, crouched behind a stone wall, some of the don's élite friends garbed in their full-sleeved, white-silk shirts and fancy britches were merely going through the motions of trading shots with the distant enemy.

Johnny Chavez sneered, then smiled grimly.

The siege was going well, he mused. The defenders' morale hadn't yet recovered from the loss of Ken Waldo and the disappearance of Morgan, believed also dead. With the concealed cannon hammering big twenty-pound balls into a weakened section of the west wall every couple of minutes, and the colonel's officers now leading their men with renewed gusto in continuing sorties, it surely could not be much longer before the final mass attack was launched.

This was to be mounted at the spot where the wall was breached. The first wave of attackers was to cross the moat by rafts which had been transported up from the town for that purpose. Of course, Moro's forces would be at their most vulnerable during the crossing — unless they got someone on the inside to lower the drawbridge for them.

Which was exactly what Chavez had long planned to do.

He was ready to make his big play. The stables' fire would shortly draw many of the defenders from their posts. With Lucetta's assistance, he was assured of effecting entry to the wheelhouse. Once inside he'd lower the bridge, the attackers would storm across and the long and bloody siege would be virtually at an end.

The plan went like clockwork.

Lucetta did exactly as he instructed and there was no resistance at the wheelhouse door when she demanded admittance 'in the name of my father.'

For the don's treacherous daughter, the grisly moment of truth came the moment Chavez followed her inside with a gun in his hand and shot the three gatemen to death before her eyes.

The girl all but passed out in horror. Her romanticized concept of rebellion had been all but bloodless: secure the gatemen, lower the drawbridge, Moro's horsemen would come charging in in great numbers and her father's surrender would be inevitable and probably immediate.

But the don's daughter had grit, and the moment she recovered from her shock she flew at a grinning Chavez with raking nails, only to be clubbed to the floor with a sixgun butt.

'Good girl,' he panted, calmly lighting a cigarillo. He sucked smoke deep into his lungs, stepped away from the blood on the floor and waited for the colonel's signal before lowering the bridge.

★ ★ ★

Caught out of arm's reach of his carbine when the wide shouldered

190

gringo in Mexican rig loomed up through the roiling tendrils of cannon smoke, the sentry propped then froze upon realizing just who it was coming towards him.

'Mother of God and Jesus protect!' he gasped fervently.

Then he darted a hand inside his dusty gray tunic, dark eyes rolling bright and sick in their sockets. The pearl-handled .38 came out very fast, much faster than Morgan expected. Yet the Mexican's big moment proved to be just that — a moment. Gunflame belched from Morgan's roaring .45 and a soft-nosed slug hit the man, hard and deep. Hitting dirt, the trooper floundered like a drowning fish, dying. Morgan stepped over the body and went low, waiting like a big crouched animal to see if the gunblast would draw attention. It didn't.

Such was the uproar of concerted gunfire from the encircling forces up here in the redoubts surrounding the hacienda, where Moro was waiting until the assault had softened the defence sufficiently before he ordered the final attack, that the shadowy figures in gray were too excited and intent on their tasks to note the incongruity of a pistol-shot punctuating the cacophony of rifle fire.

Morgan began breathing more easily.

He reloaded and squinted upslope. The bulk of one of the don's hunting-lodges blocked his view of the besieged hacienda at this point, but he could see the repeating yellow firebursts of the colonel's cannon which was rapidly chewing great holes in the perimeter walls as the assault continued unabated.

The head-jarring racket couldn't help but remind a man of Shiloh and Chancellorsville.

Upon first getting clear of the town he had intended to select the quietest-seeming sector of the gray ring encircling the hacienda, infiltrate the enemy lines at that point, swim the moat and hope his men recognized him and threw him a rope before someone shot him to doll-rags. He'd reckoned the odds against him surviving such a reckless plan to be slim at best but was still prepared to chance his arm in the desperate hope of getting back inside to assume command. The defenders were plainly faltering badly now without his hand on the tiller.

It was as he drew ever closer to the cannon position that he sighted flames licking the hacienda's southern sector not far from the gunpowder supplies. Muffling a curse, he edged around further through the brush and glimpsed what Moro's cannon was doing to the walls.

That accursed cannon! He'd thought he'd wrecked it once, only to have it come back and haunt him — haunt them all. But, calm again in an instant, he stared reality straight in the eye. He must silence that bawling bellowing piece of ordnance or the game would surely be lost.

On the positive side, sloppy security

surrounding the emplacement had already enabled him to get in much closer than he might have dared hope. He could glimpse men laughing and dancing excitedly as though they believed the circus was already over. He had news for them.

Snake-wriggling up the last slope, keeping the bulk of the hunting-lodge between himself and the cannon site, he was congratulating himself on his continuing good fortune when something slashed into the earth so close to his face that he was peppered with dirt and a stone chip gashed his cheek.

The rifle bullet that had nearly claimed him had not come from a trooper's rifle but rather from the northwestern ramparts of the hacienda!

Staring up, he had the suspicion that the bullet had almost certainly come from a mercenary's Spencer carbine; he recognized the spang of the weapon.

While his appreciation of irony might be as keen as the next man's, he had no intention of courting the ultimate irony of being slaughtered by one of his own men, and promptly changed direction to kick his way around toward the west flank of the hacienda.

So it was quite by chance that he happened upon a row of barrels occupying the porch of the hunting-lodge, each barrel clearly marked with the international symbol for high explosives!

The gunpowder for the cannon!

For a moment his heart leapt with excitement, but only for a moment. For that was all the time it took for him to realize first, there were guards in place on the lodge porch, and second, from this high point he could see down into the cannon emplacement. He realized that, even though Moro's security all over the battlefield must be poor to lousy to have let him get this far, the pit itself was fairly bristling with manpower and weaponry.

A rough count put the number of gray tunics at a score at least, some engaged in servicing the squat and ugly twenty-five-pounder, while other soldiers stood guard with still others organizing arms and ammunition on the back rim of the dugout, as though perhaps preparing for a final charge at any moment.

In addition, an even larger party of reserves was dimly visible to the rear.

Morgan fingered his Colt as he focused upon a squat figure sporting a braided billed cap and ornate shoulder epaulets. It had to be Moro! He could put a bullet through the man's brain from right where he stood, he knew. But Clay Morgan had no stomach for suicide. Cutting loose from here, he'd be chopped into dog's meat before Moro hit dirt.

Instead he began backing up towards the moat as soldiers started across from the cannon, obviously sent to fetch more gunpowder for the charges. He immediately surrendered any foolhardy hope of being able to take the cannon out of action. But he would not leave empty-handed. There was a weakness here — had to be. He wanted to find it and exploit it before making his try to get across the moat.

Ducking and dodging between the bunkers beneath a low-hanging canopy of smoke, it proved relatively easy, if a tad hard on a man's nervous system, to gain a spot on the quieter side of the northern flank within maybe a hundred yards of fortress St Leque.

The flames from the stable were by now consuming the timber and part of the brickwork of a high parapet. Cinders were raining down. He glimpsed firefighters dashing to and fro against the dramatic backdrop of leaping yellow tongues of flame. Voices came floating down out of the chaos and he thought he recognized Buck's. One thing was for sure. If Buck Clooney was still alive he'd be leading and giving orders.

Yet again the cannon sounded, the ball striking a high turret a glancing blow which caused a huge pile of loosened stone and masonry to come plunging down into the moat, sending up great geysers of spray.

By the time the spray had settled, Morgan was within twenty yards of the moat and still sprinting like a lightweight. Someone howled in back of him and rifles began to snarl. But by then he was airborne, launching himself in an enormous headlong dive, soaring through the polluted air and bellowing in a cannon-like voice: 'Morgan!' before plunging deep and ploughing onwards with a powerful overhand stroke.

Had they heard him? Would they believe it was him? The uncertainty kept him swimming underwater for far longer than he should have. Then he shot upwards with such involuntary force that he reared into full sight as far as below waist level — with not a single shot coming down from above.

He was to learn later that scarcely any of the defenders had even heard his bull-bellow as he'd dived in. It was his size that saved him. Viewed from above, it seemed his six-feet-five and 200 pound dimensions made him appear about twice the size of any soldier in this army or any other south of the border.

Even as he began stroking he was bawling orders to the staring figures above. But so certain had Buck Clooney been of his identity that he already had men dangling down from ramparts and apertures.

He'd chosen his entry spot well. It was almost dark at this point where he was coming in, and though the enemy was by now laying in an ever increasing fire, sensing who it might be even if they couldn't see him from lower down, Morgan was relying heavily on the assumption that what a man could not see he couldn't hit.

So it proved.

He was winded, bleeding, dragged down by soaked clothing and almost totally exhausted by the time strong hands reached down and quickly hauled him to safety behind the barricades. Yet he knew he had never felt better. A man always did when he pulled off the impossible or even the simply idiotic.

A beaming familiar face leaned close to his own. 'Morg, you're out of your head.'

Buck Clooney's fifty-years-old homey mug had never looked more welcome. But naturally Morgan didn't say so. When he'd recovered sufficiently for conversation he told them about the cannon and its proximity to a huge cache of gunpowder.

9

THE SIEGE

The sturdy walls of Hacienda St Leque's grand hall managed successfully to blot out most of those ugly and aggressive sounds which rose and fell with murderous regularity outside.

The orchestra was playing a slow waltz as Don Julius crossed the greased and waxed dance floor, extending a white-gloved hand to his doña who rose from her chair and blushed with pleasure at his gallantry. Then, almost completely anaesthetized by the liquor and drugs she imbibed to steady her nerves, yet still physically functional and graceful, she moved toward her partner, curtsying, rising and extending both hands for his grasp.

Polite applause came from all sides, and now Don Julius and Doña Iselda were gliding around in stately graceful circles, protocol decreed that other dancers were free to take to the floor, which they did in numbers.

As though in a desperate attempt to cover up their dismay and sense of the impending doom which they believed would come when that infernal cannon ceased its barrage, and the gray hordes of Moro's regiment came swarming across the moat like so many beasts ravening for the kill, the *ricos* had dressed in their very finest for this occasion.

Silks and satins were to be seen in abundance as were shimmering jewels and brave displays of various medals and honors.

The string quintet played well with only the occasional bad note to hint at just how tense and terrified the musicians really were behind their starched shirtfronts and square-shouldered black jackets. But nothing could prevent dancers, diners, musicians or bustling table staff from sneaking quick and wide-eyed glances at the tall arched doors which remained reassuringly closed against the smoke from the fires and the relentless snarl of the battle.

'You dance very well this evening, madame.'

'As do you yourself, señor. What a pity it is not a little cooler.'

'Ah yes. But remember, a little humidity only adds to the pleasure of the wine on such an occasion.'

'You are as wise as always, Don Julius.'

The condemned ate a hearty meal.

That was how a cynic might have viewed the scene when, after the dancing ceased, the long tables were set out in the center of the hall and the guests sat down to as fine a meal as the kitchens of St Leque had ever produced.

Why not empty pantry and cellar if this were indeed to prove to be the last supper?

Smiling and chatting they attacked the viands heartily and washed them down with delicate rosé wines imported all the way from Seville. They talked feverishly and ate greedily. Occasionally an elegantly dressed woman in pearls and dew-drop earrings of solid silver might start involuntarily at the crump of the accursed cannon. But diners pretended not to notice and a discreet servant might subtly slip a straight double brandy to the woman in case the wine wasn't deadening her senses quite as effectively as it might be expected to do.

Glancing around, a diner might not glimpse a single solemn countenance. And yet, there was not a guest present who didn't know the end was near.

During the years of his total dominion over the valley and its rich and poor, Don Julius had been the symbol of power and authority. Even in the wake of Moro's catastrophic takeover of Moritomo Valley which had compelled the don and his army of friends, sycophants, relatives and hangers-on to fort up here in the grand hacienda,

Diaz had continued to command unquestioned authority. He had once again proved an inspiration to all both in the great hall and out on the barricades tonight. He remained the force of hope in their overturned, fear-ridden lives.

The don's court had always believed that the day would come when Moro would fall, the siege would be lifted and Diaz would lead them all triumphantly across the drawbridge to resume their powerful, pleasure filled lives as rulers of the valley again.

Not any longer.

One only had to study the man behind the arrogant mask seated at the head of the great table now to know that it was all a sham, that Armageddon was truly at hand. The certain death of Morgan in whom they had all placed such trust followed by the enemy's all-out assault on the hacienda fortress tonight — all had combined to shatter Don Julius's brittle, vainglorious spirit and reduce him to the ranks of lesser men.

Yet even many of those who could see through the don's veneer were unexpectedly impressed by his lady as she sat serene and smiling at his side as if nothing untoward had happened, concerned only, so it seemed, that the second violinist seemed a tad off-key, and only registering mild concern that her daughter and her young man were still to join them.

A combination of shock, drugs and a deepening psychosis was protecting Doña Iselda Diaz from the reality that was slowly but surely tearing the don apart.

The more perceptive amongst those present may have realized that the Diazes were slowly collapsing before their eyes, yet they showed no pity. What pity these *ricos* had left in them by now was lavished exclusively upon themselves.

'Why hasn't Mexico City intervened by this?' a stiff-necked financier asked querulously.

While the wealthy horse-breeder and dealer wanted to know: 'Are there any contingency plans should these scoundrels actually succeed in breaching our walls? Doesn't anybody know?'

'God alone knows, Señor Raimirez,' Iselda broke in unexpectedly, her manner suddenly as melancholy as it had been happy mere moments before. 'But God, of course, has abandoned us, can't you see? God has forgotten His own.'

'Enough of that, Iselda,' the don chided automatically. He turned sharply to focus upon the servants by the main doors. 'Any sign of Señorita Lucetta?'

Heads shook silently and Diaz turned back to the table. 'She knows we do not tolerate tardiness,' he said as though everyday conventions still applied on this night of high drama and threatening chaos. 'Enrique and Paolo, go and find the princess and bring her here immediately.'

'And tell her mama loves her!' Iselda called as the men rose and made for the double doors. 'And do ask Mr Morgan to look in on us. I am sure you will find him on the battlements, leading by example as always.'

'Morgan is *muerto*, *señora*!' Diaz snapped. He gestured dramatically. 'Slain by Moro on his foolish attempt to assassinate the evil one and then torn to pieces by the devil birds upon the gibbet as we saw with our own eyes. Cannot you digest that simple fact? The gringo you seduced into coming here is dead and it is thanks to his recklessness we are in this peril. Do you understand what I say?'

Before Iselda could respond, a ricocheting bullet smashed through a high window, showering a side-table and two servants with silvery shards of glass.

The music stopped.

Everyone stared at the window. Up until that moment they had been able to maintain the façade of normality deep within this most secure section of the hacienda which they had considered impregnable . . . until now.

Suddenly a woman began to scream. She pointed to Iselda. 'She is right! She is right! God has forsaken us!' She waved her arms at the men gathered about the table. 'How can you sit there drinking and talking as though nothing is wrong? They are going to murder us!'

She swung wildly on the pale don.

'What can we do, Don Julius? Tell us all what we can do.'

But the don had no answers, solutions or plans of battle. He stared dully into his goblet of wine, oblivious to the woman's wild sobbing or his wife's renewed distraction. He seemed dazed to the reality of their vulnerability.

At that moment the tall doors burst open and Enrique and Paolo burst into the room, wide-eyed and breathless.

Their search for Lucetta had brought an astonishing result. Defenders in the bridge yard had reported that Lucetta and Johnny Chavez had somehow entered the bridgehouse half an hour earlier. They had locked the security gate from the inside and nothing had been seen of the couple or the drawbridge operators since.

The news had a dramatic effect. It seemed almost as though Don Julius had been waiting for something like this to jolt him out of the lethargy and dejection that had overcome him over the past minutes.

Suddenly he was on his feet looking almost like his old self.

'She has no business being in the bridgehouse — especially at such a critical time. As for Chavez . . . '

His voice trailed away. In his sharpened, reawakened state, Don Julius was suddenly reviewing in his mind all the little, seemingly unimportant things about Johnny Chavez which he had never liked or didn't seem to understand. This added to his sense of urgency as he kicked away his high-backed Spanish chair and struck a dramatic pose.

'There is something very wrong about what we have just learned, *compañeros*!' he cried in a voice that

carried. 'They might destroy my hacienda but none shall ever harm our
daughter. Quickly, we go below, all of
us. We shall arm ourselves, men and
women alike, and if our beloved
daughter is in danger we shall save her
— not the gringos or our *bravos* on the
walls — but us, the brave élite!'

It was an inspirational call to arms
— it was also a command and not a
request from a man they had reason to
fear even more than the enemy outside.

The rush for the tall doors emptied
the room in mere moments until only
Iselda Diaz remained, fixed to her seat,
unable to comprehend what had just
taken place. It was only when she heard
a departing guest cry: 'Save Lucetta!'
that the mental fog lifted and she was
up and rushing for the wide-open
doors.

'Lucetta, we are coming!' she screamed.
And then, 'Summon Clay Morgan to
lead us!'

Her husband shot her a scornful look
over his shoulder as he led the glittering

crowd for the spiral staircase, while others traded significant stares and one dowager in pearls made a circular motion with her finger at her temple.

'Crazy' Iselda as she had come to be known increasingly in the last week, had plainly lost her last grip on reality, it seemed.

Yet even as the crowd gained the level below and went surging across the courtyard by the blazing barn, they were assailed by the news they might have heard earlier had not Diaz forbidden any news, either good or bad, to intrude on what he had secretly expected to be his last great banquet, perhaps the end of everything for him.

Morgan was alive! He'd just swum the moat to rejoin his mercenaries and right at that moment was directing the defence from the east balcony!

Upon hearing this the don began to weep tears of relief, for in the time he'd been here the big gunman had added a stiffening to the defence that he'd considered impossible, as well as showing himself a master tactician.

'*Viva Morgan!*' he howled, and the cry was taken up to become a chant that rocked the battle-scarred walls and rolled across the dark and smoky waters of the moat to reach the enemy in his dugouts and emplacements, confirming what they had only half-guessed before, namely that big Morgan who'd quit the security of the hacienda to challenge them upon their home turf earlier, had eluded the massive search for him in Ascension, had later apparently attempted a one-man assault to wreck their cannon — and now had survived the moat and was once more leading the resistance!

Tears of relief and rage spilled from the don's eyes as he yelled and gesticulated at his men, displaying the genuine fighting spirit which he had only feigned before. Immediately he was envisioning a heroic Morgan-led counter-attack which would leave the accursed Moro's forces routed and scattered, his own return to total power assured.

And sweet revenge against every one of his misbegotten enemies, and the lash and in some cases the firing squad for all the treacherous peons who had turned away from him and joined Moro in the battle for Valley Moritomo.

Dispatching a runner to order Morgan and his men to join them at the bridge-house, the rejuvenated Don Julius led his retainers down the broad stone staircase to ground level, pistol in hand, chest inflated, hero of the final battle as good as won.

But when the runner reached the south compound, neither Morgan nor any of his men were anywhere to be seen.

★   ★   ★

The wind blew more strongly up here on the highest turret on the hacienda's eastern side. The height advantage offered the mercenaries a vastly improved view of the encircling enemy's positions beyond the moat at this point.

They could see at a glance that the bulk of the siege-men were now assembled behind cover just beyond rifle range in the timbered draw in back of the cannon emplacement hard by the don's hunting-lodge.

Eyes cut to slits as he played his gaze over the battlefield, Morgan took his time loading the high-powered rifle in his hands before making his summary:

'The way they keep increasing the cannon fire,' so he pointed out to Clooney, Crazy Jake, Dundee and the rest, 'tells us they're softening us up in the drawbridge sector for another assault there. And those troopers I came close to falling over in back of the cannon, along with the others that have joined them since I got across, add up to the same conclusion. Moro means to send them in again in numbers.'

'Into the moat, Morg?' Clooney queried.

'That,' conceded Morgan, 'is where

my figuring breaks down.'

Leaning forward with the glow of small fires touched off by the cannon fire tinting his broad cheekbones, he switched his attention to focus upon the upraised drawbridge and wheelhouse directly below.

'Looks all shipshape down there,' he conceded as he leaned back, wide-shouldered and grim-jawed against the troubled sky. 'Which doesn't make sense — attackwise, that is. Moro might be a whoremaster's pimp and a murdering son of a bitch, but he's proved he's no fool. So . . . what's his play?'

Nobody answered for the moment. Their opinions were rarely sought by their trail boss. Not on anything.

First to recover from his surprise, Buck Clooney said: 'You reckon that mebbe this big attack he's buildin' up to might be just a diversion, Morg, somethin' to take our attention off of the real play someplace else?'

'Could be.'

Deadly gunmen stared. If it was strange for Morgan to seek the opinion of others it was almost unheard of for him to concede that anyone apart from Clay Morgan himself might have a notion halfway worth considering.

Was the veteran of the gun going soft?

Morgan pondered that himself, just as he was trying to figure why he couldn't get Soledad Engracia out of his mind despite an unfolding drama which would normally preoccupy him one hundred per cent. For if ever a man needed a crystal clear and unencumbered thinkbox, it was now.

'Or could be mebbe them chocolate soldiers are plannin' to swim that fool moat like you done?' suggested Clooney.

'Yeah . . . mebbe . . . ' Morgan replied vaguely.

It was only then that his men realized that Morgan was not really soliciting opinions at all. In fact it seemed he wasn't even listening to what was said.

His gaze, they noted, was no longer

directed at the scene below but rather was focused on the distant blinking lights of the town up-valley. Maybe that in itself was hardly alarming. But might not any man have been jolted to his very bootstraps had he realized that, maybe for the first time in his memory, Morgan was aware he was afraid to die.

Death had never meant much to him one way or another. But something had surely changed him. No, not Iselda. He'd looked into that handsome lady's troubled eyes that first day and realized any foolish dream he might have had of him and her had been destroyed by something he didn't fully understand.

Which left only Soledad Engracia.

She was the first woman he'd ever encountered who treated him like a man with strengths and weaknesses and not as some kind of coffin-filler with ice-water in his veins.

And this romantic thought — so grossly inappropriate at that life-or-death moment — affected Clay Morgan in a way most of them had never seen before.

He was smiling.

This had the effect of startling these lean-hipped and lantern-jawed wolves of the gun, and their bemused expressions all asked the same question. Had big Morgan maybe signed up for one assignment too many?

He caught their looks, reacted in pure Morgan style. 'Ten . . . hut!' he barked, causing a couple to start, and in the instant there was not a puzzled expression to be seen. If he'd stepped out of character for a moment, he was well and truly back in classic Morgan mode almost instantly. It showed in his every inch, every hard word.

'Now listen up and get this straight,' he ordered, setting his rifle up on the parapet, ready to fire. He pointed. 'That building out there you can just see the flank of is stuffed window-high with gunpowder. We can't hit it clean from here, our slugs would just glance off. So, what we're going to do is aim instead for that big slab of talus leaning up at an angle on the slope side of the building. We're going to direct our fire at that about ten feet up from ground level and hope we luck a ricochet that will drill into the back porch wall and touch off the explosives. Any questions?'

If they had any, they were smart enough to keep them to themselves.

For they all knew Morgan well enough to know he wasn't in the mood for any more talk. He wanted action, and as the cannon boomed and chewed another big bite out of the hacienda's lower walls, they were ready to give him what he wanted.

Soon high-powered rifles were to be seen flaring and snarling from the lofted position and for some time neither friend nor foe could figure what they were shooting at.

* * *

A rotund silhouette materialized from the gloom beyond the cell door, and the voice that issued from its bulk was soft, cultivated and mocking.

'You wish for the sacraments, my son?'

The lean prisoner had trouble focusing his gaze. He was recovering from a fever and the light was never better than gloomy in the cells, passageways and spider-haunted niches of Rio Toro jail.

'What?'

Damaron's voice sounded strange to his own ears. He'd just finished ten days in solitary, where he had contracted, fought and ultimately survived his bout of river fever.

'You remember me, my son. I am the bringer of the Word.'

Damaron cursed. He attempted to dredge up saliva to spit but his mouth was too dry. He settled for calling the priest the eunuch son of the whore of Babylon, tried to reach that fat neck through the bars, but his weak arm was easily brushed aside.

'So much fire, so little intelligence,' mocked the priest whose occasional

221

visits to this cesspit of a prison were more for his own personal entertainment than demonstrations of ministering zeal. 'But be not guilty, my son, as your *padre* understands your weakness of mind, body and soul. Besides, I bring you news to cheer you.'

'You got cancer?'

Something close to admiration glinted briefly in the priest's rogue eyes. For he had been on hand from time to time to witness the gringo Damaron's defiance, suffering and raw courage as he battled with his jailers, the prison, his destiny. Having seen the prisoner absorb so much brutal punishment, the *padre* had come to suspect that it was hatred that made Flash Damaron strong and kept him alive. And he was right.

'The fight to the death continues in Valley Moritomo,' the *padre* informed. He smiled, a moonfaced young man with the hypnotic stare of an illusionist. 'Yesterday I heard that your *bête noir*, Morgan, had perished. But before I could reach you with this good news, alas, I was informed that by some miracle he had survived and was back at Hacienda St Leque leading the struggle against the great and just Colonel Moro.'

Damaron's once handsome face tilted forwards and was lost in shadow. His eyes burned cold. His jailers accused him of being crazed with hate. They taunted him about what he had been once and what he had now become. Most times he ignored them. Other times he retaliated violently and was hurled back into the hole which would require considerable upgrading even to qualify as a latrine.

Each time he emerged from solitary he was crazier, more defiant and more committed than ever to his one goal in life.

Kill Morgan.

* * *

Lucetta Diaz moaned softly, rolled on to her back and at last opened her eyes.

Consciousness brought awareness of the sharp pain in her temple and pain brought recollection.

Chavez!

Closing her eyes to mere slits, she risked turning her head slightly to one side. This movement brought into her line of vision the sprawled and bloodied corpses of the bridgehouse guards; beyond them, crouched by the chain slots overlooking moat and battleground, was Johnny Chavez. His back was turned to her and his every inch reflected his intensity as he waited, hand on lever, for Moro's signal from across the moat, telling him when to lower the bridge. Obviously no psychic sense disturbed his concentration or warned him she had regained consciousness; he appeared blissfully unaware of the twin beams of pure hatred drilling from her staring eyes into his slender back.

Although the princess had convinced herself that she loved Chavez and his cause, what she had always done best and most naturally was hate. She was one of those people to whom love came almost impossibly hard, yet hate flowed as smoothly and readily as water.

Her hatred at that moment was unprecedented in its intensity and more than sufficiently powerful for her to shrug off the remaining effects of the brutal blow to the head she had sustained. She found herself able to ignore the vast spread of blood across the floor as well as the locked-eyed corpses, and begin dragging herself stealthily towards a dropped and fully loaded .45.

Nobody could betray her and survive. Nobody!

Abruptly she paused. Only now was she growing aware of the sounds of shouting from beyond the sturdy locked doors, shouting that was loud enough to make itself heard above the gunfire and the screams of the dying.

Her parents!

They were just outside and calling to be let in. Lucetta flicked her gaze at Chavez's back again. The young man remained absorbed, and with good reason.

The all-important attack he'd been waiting for was overdue.

What in hell was Moro doing out there?

* * *

The colonel cursed as yet another howling ricochet completely missed its target, the lodge, flew upslope, then spanged off the fat barrel of his squat gray cannon, causing his grenadiers to duck.

In back of Moro, some hundred yards distant, was his massed, waiting attack force; ahead of him was the brooding, smoke-wreathed bulk of the hacienda, the moat and the upraised drawbridge.

He'd received Chavez's agreed-upon first signal from the bridgehouse twenty minutes earlier. It informed the colonel that Chavez was now in position to lower the drawbridge just as soon as the colonel led his troops from behind the cover of the ridge and the hunting lodge and upslope to the moat, then gave him the agreed signal to drop the bridge and let the invasion begin.

The reason for the delay in the attack was now clear.

Ever since Morgan's dramatic return to the hacienda, the resistance had stepped up remarkably, culminating in the continuing volleys from the heights of the besieged fortress which were harrying the soldiers and raising the spectre of an explosion should so much as just one bullet ricochet off the talus at just the right angle and penetrate the powder-filled lodge.

Moro would have liked to postpone his rush to the moat to a more propitious moment, yet he dared not. For the daring Chavez had upheld his risky part of their agreement in securing access to the bridgehouse, an advantage they would never get again were they to hold back now.

And yet Colonel Moro continued to

do what for him was highly uncharacteristic. He vacillated. He didn't call off the assault but neither did he unleash it. Every sure instinct told him that he must win this battle and overrun St Leque, right now, tonight, or the tide must surely run against him. But how murderously costly might that success prove to be with that lethal hail of bullets scything down upon them from directly above — even if the enemy had failed in their obvious purpose to touch off his gunpowder cache.

The colonel cursed impotently, ground his teeth, called God's or Satan's wrath down upon Morgan's head — then suddenly something clicked within him and he was once again calm, ice-cool and thinking strategically.

That volleying from the high spot above the watchtower was doing all the damage and forcing him to delay his attack. But he had a cannon — so why was he not using it to best advantage?

It was the bravo Colonel Moro of old who suddenly sprang to his feet and went zigzagging across the mercifully short space of open country with vicious leaden hornets instantly zipping and droning about his weaving figure. A bullet smashed off the heel of his right boot causing his entire leg to go briefly numb. The colonel dived left, rolled right, caught his breath as a two-ounce slug of whispering death fanned his cheek, then he was diving full length off the ridge, to go rolling and somersaulting down the wooded slope and out of sight of the hawk-eyed riflemen trying so hard to murder him.

His heart hammered as he halted to regain his breath. Then he was afoot and limping swiftly around the lower side of the sturdy hunting-lodge to reach the cannon emplacement, where he breathlessly ordered the sweating, smoke-blackened cannoneers to raise and alter their line of fire once more.

They obeyed with the alacrity he'd drilled into them, and their first blast at the high turret chewed out a tenfoot length of wall and hurled at least one cartwheeling body into the sky.

Tears of excitement ran down Moro's cheeks as he sprang to his feet to pluck from inside his tunic the crimson sash. Now that the vicious fire from above was momentarily halted, all he must do was give the prearranged signal to Chavez in the wheelhouse to activate the bridge mechanism, then lead his men up and over the no longer dangerous slope to be on hand and ready to cross the moat the moment the drawbridge came thudding down.

He was roaring in anticipation when a bullet struck a tree nearby, flattened out from the impact, fluttered across the heads of his cannoneers with a sound like a demented bee, smacked the colonel in the temple and knocked him unconscious to the ground.

★   ★   ★

She got the pistol in her hands and even managed to cock it. But even that small warning sound of the hammer going back was picked up by a hyper-alert Chavez, who came wheeling out of his bucket-chair to snatch the .45 from her hand. He backhanded her across the face before she could do more than scream.

The sound carried.

The banging upon the locked doors and shouting increased sharply. They were still out there — her parents and God alone knew how many others. Whipping one arm about the girl's throat, Chavez propelled her through the second doorway into the small flagged courtyard, where they were visible through the unmanned gunports.

'Surrender the hacienda or she dies, Don Julius!' he shouted. 'I mean what I say. Make your decision now!'

Stunned but defiant, a white-faced Diaz shook his head stubbornly and backed away from the gunports. He was aghast at the situation but could not do as commanded. Not give up everything when victory might well prove achievable simply because of a foolish daughter and the crisis into which her headstrong nature had plainly led her.

He could not. Would not. *Madre de Dios* — no!

Suddenly he found himself attacked from behind. He whirled to confront the madwoman.

'Do as he says!' screamed his wife, tearing at his face with raking nails. 'What is the hacienda or victory against our beloved — '

Her voice was swallowed by a crumpling roar of sound. One hundred feet above, tons of masonry, timber and iron that had been the high vantage point upon which Morgan's snipers had been barricaded and from where they had been inflicting such damage upon the enemy, were thundering down into the patios and courtyards below as the redirected cannon found the right line and range.

There followed a moment's stunned and dramatic silence.

Only minutes earlier one of the don's lackeys had tracked down Morgan and his band to that parapet. The don had immediately dispatched a messenger ordering Morgan to bring his men to the bridgehouse to help deal with the crisis there. There had been no sign of the mercenaries. Now surely the Yankee gunmen were no more.

The stunned silence was broken by a mighty cheer from the enemy ranks; Moro's men were cheering their cannoneer's accuracy.

Fifteen feet distant, an elated Johnny Chavez whirled back into the bridgehouse, hauling his hostage after him. He was just in time to catch a flash of a fluttering scarf from the hunting-lodge porch where a recovered Moro had at least managed to get his signal away — the all-important signal that told his accomplice-in-arms that the long-delayed attack was about to begin.

Laughing almost hysterically, Chavez seized the levers and heaved his weight upon them. Mighty wheels groaned and the rattle of massive chains was deafening in the confined space. Slowly the heavy drawbridge began to come down, revealing the yawning cavern of the entranceway to Moro and his gray swarm of fighting men now rushing up the bullet-torn slope from the lodge.

Behind their scarred and battered walls the don and his men stood as though rooted to the spot. The mercenaries were dead and the enemy was rushing towards the by now swiftly falling drawbridge. Dumb, disbelieving, they began backing away, scarcely any man among them lifting a weapon to defend himself, pampered and over-protected little men facing the final disaster, caring only for themselves and ready to surrender their small lives like sheep before the slaughtermen.

And drowning out even the sounds of approaching disaster could be heard the agonized wailing for her daughter of the doña, which cut off as though someone had thrown a switch as the woman lurched blindly towards a nearby stairwell — and saw Clay Morgan emerge from it.

Morgan should have been dead. Would certainly have been had not Don Julius's summons reached his party above and sent them headlong down the staircase mere moments before Moro's cannoneers blew their fortified position into the sky.

Their descent to ground level was delayed further by falling debris, but that only served to make their eventual appearance all the more dramatic. They had survived. But for how long? The drawbridge was almost down by the time the last fighter cleared the stairwell, with Moro, whipped up to full fighting mode, leading over the last few racing yards.

In moments the enemy would be across the bridge and into the hacienda that had denied them entry for so long.

Morgan shot a look at his men as he filled both hands with Colts, his brave, mercenary damn-you-to-hell boys, and he saw in every face what he expected to see, what he knew would be there.

Courage, loyalty and the readiness to

die with as much fierce distinction as they'd lived.

He murmured the name of a woman none of them knew of as he signalled to them to follow him. He led them around the curved flank of the wheel-house to mount the now horizontal drawbridge in the same moment as its opposite end thudded into its massive cradles and the first snarling enemy rushed headlong on to it.

Buck Clooney killed that first man with his first shot and so it began — one thin gringo line standing against a rushing gray horde.

But what a line it was!

For a handful of crimson moments it appeared that the defenders must go down before the human tide. But they didn't. Men fell, some to lie still, but others to keep triggering from the kneeling or lying position, blasting with such murderous effectiveness that the enemy charge first faltered, struggled mightily to hold, but gave way again and in sections began to crumble.

An American voice raised a cheer. The sound sent tingling down the spines of lesser men, even the least of them all as represented by the don and what was left of his court.

The don astonished himself and his people when he whipped out a chased-silver pistol everyone thought was purely ornamental and drilled a bull-roaring buck sergeant clean between the eyes with it.

Down on one knee with blood seeping from a flesh wound, Morgan saw the sergeant go down and in doing so expose the by now fearful figure of Moro, who had been so quick to scent victory and was now even quicker to catch the first rancid whiff of defeat.

Morgan's bullet hit the colonel somewhere low down. He howled and was attempting to bring up his long-barrel when another bullet came looking for him. It thudded home and the man went down with the roar of battle dimming in his ears, never feeling the boots running over him as the mercenary-led fightback stormed right over him to pour shot after shot into the backs of men now running for their lives.

Moments later, Clooney was hit. Morgan whirled to support the man, and as he did glimpsed movement in the vicinity of the wheelhouse as Johnny Chavez made a reckless run for it, using Lucetta Diaz as his shield.

The couple made it as far as the central courtyard with the girl screaming wildly, Chavez thrusting the gun barrel into her neck, onlookers too afraid for her life to intervene. But suddenly a woman broke from the crowd and threw herself screaming at Chavez, who was taken by surprise by the lightning attack.

It was Doña Iselda.

Somehow the demented woman managed to bring the man to ground. Instantly the don and several men rushed in to assist the Doña. But Chavez was too fast, too furiously intent on being a survivor no matter how many scores might perish here. His flaming revolver cut Diaz down in his tracks and in the same insane instant he whipped his gun around and drove a bullet into Lucetta's back as the girl tried to flee the slaughter.

Unsighted momentarily, Morgan knew it was the girl who had died by the way the mother screamed, a sound straight out of hell.

Triumphant, lightning-fast, Chavez regained his feet and was bunching his leg-muscles to explode away when for just a moment out of eternity he was exposed to the guns of Dundee, Chiller and Morgan.

The mercenaries' combined fire came in almost the same instant in a great shout of sound that sounded more like Moro's cannon than three sixshooters from north of the border.

Reloading, iron-jawed and implacable now, Morgan led his battered but still resolute brigade off through the flames and gunsmoke to cross the bridge, intent on throwing himself with them into the battle still raging along that body-littered slope.

Suddenly he halted and the gunmen stopped at his side. They were staring, uncomprehendingly at first, as the brush below that bloodied battle-scene suddenly came alive with a swarming tide of howling human figures in off-white shirts and pants, crude sandals and big straw-hats.

The myth of the peasants' revolt, conceived by Chavez to mislead Lucetta Diaz, had actually become a reality.

The mercenaries had first crippled the snake of the gray oppressors. Now the poor and the hungry and the suddenly courageous were rushing in for the final kill.

It seemed an eternity to a motionless, blank-faced Morgan before he realized that the last shot had been fired and the terrible screaming had ceased.

10

SILENT GROW THE GUNS

The Royal Commissar of the Emperor's Armies stood before the giant colored wall-map of the Northern Provinces, cigarette-holder jutting from between strong teeth, one eyebrow clamped down over the eye in concentration while the other arched high to convey an impression of world-weary cynicism bordering on total indifference.

'So what exactly is the present situation in that benighted valley, General? And do be brief. I am expected at the palace. We may shortly be at war with Nicaragua.'

The general cleared his throat hurriedly.

'Intelligence informs us that the survivors of Moro's forces have been driven out and the peons have totally taken over. *Madre de Dios!* Such a hotbed of trouble! Just months ago Don Julius ruled unchallenged and all was wonderful. Then the corrupt and ambitious Moro embarked upon his mission of conquest, and now un-washed peasant scum have dominion there. They — '

'What of the gringo mercenaries?'

The general rustled his papers and peered through his monocle at the relevant document.

'Many of them were slain in the final battle, sire . . . '

'What of the leader, Morgan?'

The Royal Commissar kept inter-rupting. He genuinely was anxious to get to the palace before the unstable emperor went completely loco and declared war on some country like England or Spain. And even without such pressing matters to contend with, he could really not care less about overblown aristocrats and corrupt army officers squabbling over the spoils in some God-forsaken dustbowl at the far northern edge of the province. In his opinion, the only contribution of such people to life in Mexico City was to churn up troubles and give him an administrative pain in the rear end. He snapped his fingers. 'Alive, I assume?'

Again the portly general consulted his documents. 'There is no record of his death, Excellency. But how did you know that?'

'Men like Morgan never die when they really should, or when you really wish they would. That has been my experience with that accursed gringo breed. The Devil looks after his own.' He shrugged eloquently, resignedly. 'So now we have yet another regime in power in Valley Moritomo and in all probability enough survivors from the mercenary force to make any attempted military takeover by us difficult if not impossible, even if we had the resources to attempt such a thing. Is that a correct assessment of the situation?'

'Ahh . . . I believe so, sire.'

With that the Royal Commissar promptly snatched the documents from the general's pudgy hands and tossed them into the wicker wastebasket.

The general stared. But there was no need for words. The commissar's actions were eloquent enough. With one decisive action here in this quiet and orderly office, Valley Moritomo had been consigned to whatever fate it might suffer under the administration of a tribe of uneducated and unwashed peons and likely at least a handful of bloody-handed Arizona backshooters.

There was no logical reason for the Royal Commissar or his general to expect that Moritomo's future would be any less tumultous, violent and disastrous for its peasant population than its past had been.

It would not be the first time they were proved wrong.

★ ★ ★

Iselda said: 'Is she coming soon, my husband?'

'Lucetta?' Morgan replied. 'Yeah,

she'll be by directly.'

'She will bring me flowers . . . she always brings her mama flowers.'

'She's a fine daughter, sure enough.'

The uniformed attendant touched Morgan's shoulder. 'She grows tired, señor.'

'Yeah, guess so.'

Before quitting the white room with its crisp starched curtains and sunlight streaming in from the hospital orchards, he rested a hand upon the woman's shoulder, his big gunman's paw so brown against her white gown. Iselda looked up but her eyes were vacant, now as for ever.

'Send my little girl to me and I shall braid her hair. Such pretty hair.'

He bent to kiss her, then walked to the door. He paused to look back one last time. She was free now, he thought. She remembered nothing. Not that the don was dead, or that her beloved Lucetta also had been killed. Those last troubled months at the hacienda — all was mercifully erased. She was at peace.

'Have a good dream, Iselda,' he said, and was gone.

* * *

She would receive the best of care. Enough wealth had been salvaged from the hacienda to ensure that Los Lunas' finest hospital would be able to lavish the very best of treatment upon their most recent, saddest patient. But there was an additional guarantee of Iselda's future comfort. It was the gunfighter's solemn promise to 'Come back here and bust ass like you wouldn't believe,' if he should ever hear one whisper of less than total care.

And even in this place, where so many of the disturbed, violent, frightened and dangerous were housed, this huge scarred *Americano* with his double tied-down guns and deep voice rated as about the scariest thing they had ever seen.

Yet the fine treatment and quiet beauty of the asylum were as nothing to

Iselda Diaz. She existed now only in the sunlit world of her mind.

Each time they looked in on her after that they saw only a gently rocking figure in white, her lips curved in a gentle smile and her eyes unfocused, the tray of food at her side as completely forgotten as the momentous events that had spelled the end of Hacienda St Leque.

Sometimes when they tended her she might be roused to speak, either to say something about the princess or to remind them: 'Even the birds have flown away. God has forgotten His own.'

Never would she want, demand or need again. She would ask for nothing more than the white stillness of her room, waiting for her daughter to come to her.

* * *

Buck Clooney said: 'Soledad wants some cord-wood chopped, Morg. You want to oblige your wife?'

Sprawled in his big chair in the winter sun of Gabriel Valley, Clay Morgan's comfortable belly jiggled a little when he laughed out loud. Although it was several years now since she had first heard her man laugh, long after the Battle of Valley Moritomo, Soledad still thrust her head from the kitchen window at the sound, smiling today at the spectacle of two lifetime friends comfortably growing middle-aged together.

'In simple words, Clooney — that'll be the day.'

'Figgered you'd say that,' Clooney said resignedly, hefting the axe. 'Er, you don't reckon the sound of my choppin' might disturb your rest, do you?'

'Resting? You getting older but you are not getting any smarter, pilgrim.' Morgan slapped the oaken armrests. 'Right now I'm working harder than you ever looked like doing.'

'At what?'

'At enjoying life. You know a better job?'

'Guess not,' Clooney had to confess, and headed for the woodshed. But crochety as always, the now graying ex-gunslinger couldn't resist a parting shot. 'But Soledad ain't gonna be happy, you spendin' another day in that chair, boy.'

'Want to bet?'

Soledad's smooth face appeared at the kitchen window. 'What do you *hombres* argue about today?'

'He thinks you're the boss,' Morgan said. 'I just straightened him out. How's the coffee-pot going, *chiquita*?'

He had his coffee within the minute. His wife stood by the big chair and stroked his thinning hair. Every pound he gained, every hair he lost, Soledad saw as a reaffirmation of this seemingly impossibly peaceful life they enjoyed now. Her poverty and hardship were a fading memory, his calm and orderly role as rancher, stepfather and loving husband a blessed contrast to his two decades spent in the most dangerous profession of all.

If only she could be completely free of those uneasy dreams she sometimes endured, she mused. And in her imagination saw again the lean figures of phantom killers, heard again — as she had heard unforgettably in those last days in Moritomo — the crashing snarl of the guns come to haunt her here in the ongoing tranquility of Gabriel Valley.

'What is it, honey?' he said, looking up at her.

'I think I left something on the stove, *caballero*.'

'Then better go see to it.' He grinned. 'Can't have two loafers in the one family, woman.'

Her eyes told him everything as she turned to go. 'If living in peace without fear or guns is loafing, then it is my prayer you loaf all your life. In any case, your wife is young and strong . . . and I always feel your *amigos* like having you boss them around, as you do.'

He gazed across the ranchyard where Kit Chiller and Crazy Jake were breaking in a two-year-old with his children watching from the top rail of the corral, their cries of excitement reaching him above the ring of Clooney's axe.

He closed his eyes and the winter sun was warm on his face.

★   ★   ★

'Flash,' the once-husky gunman sighed wearily, 'we gotta rest up, man. Your horse is wobbly in the fetlocks, and just take a look at mine. Second City can wait another day or two, can't it? I mean, what's the hurry?'

'We can rest when we're dead,' came the harsh reply. 'In any case, we're mighty close to where we want to go.'

Wilson gazed around. They'd spent most of that day working their way through rugged hill country but now there were glimpses of wide rangelands to the north from this high stretch of trail. Years ago, this graying outlaw could have ridden twice the distance they'd covered today and still been been fit enough to drink half the night and maybe get into a fight at the end of it.

Not any more.

Nothing like five years in a Mex jail to age a man decades ahead of his time, he realized.

He studied his partner as he twisted tobacco and rice-paper into a neat cylinder. Nobody was ever likely to nickname Damaron 'Flash' now on meeting him for the first time, he mused. Sure, he might look hard as nails and was as mean as a sidewinder still, but the twenty pounds weight he'd lost, the twisted-jaw legacy from that punch an old enemy had connected him with years ago — all compounded by five years of living hell in Rio Toro had taken the gloss off Flash Damaron even if it hadn't noticeably cost him any of the old drive and restless energy.

'You still ain't told me what this great job is you've got us lined up for, Flash.'

Damaron's eyes glittered as he drew

smoke deep into his lungs. He was staring northwards as he'd been doing ever since the day they walked out of the gates of Rio Toro.

'Big job, Wilson . . . the biggest. Let's ride . . . '

They travelled on, riding Indian file through the thinning timber until reaching a clearing where they sighted a made road and the sign, which read: MORGAN RANCH 2 MILES. Wilson jerked his horse's head cruelly to bring it to a halt. 'What the blue hell!' he gasped, eyes flaring with sudden anger. 'You . . . you bastard, Flash! You planned this . . . you dirty, double-crossin' son of a b — '

'Take it easy, *amigo*. And don't cut up rough. OK, so I didn't spell it out to you, but you must've known I'd come after Morgan the day we were free.' Damaron gestured north where fenced range and a meandering creek were now visible on the plains. 'I found out where he was hanging his hat back in Cyclone — where he's been for years now . . . '

A strange excitement appeared to grip the killer now and his hand was shaking some as he reached down and caressed the handle of the Colt .45 which they'd returned to him the day they finally checked him out of Rio Toro prison.

'Just think, Wilson . . . getting square for all those years, months, days, seconds . . . the roaches and rats, the floggings and executions and — '

'And the lies!'

Wilson's cadaverous face was livid. He'd always been aware of the other's crazy hate for Morgan, which he'd seen intensify rather than lessen over the prison years. But there had never been any wild talk of revenge, of hunting the big gunfighter down once they were free. He had endured five years of hell in order that he might live — not risk his life against someone of Morgan's stature. 'Damn you, Flash,' he said, turning his horse around. 'Damn you to hell and — '

'Hold up, boy.' Damaron's tone was icy. 'I need you down there with me, mister. They told me back down in Dunsdown that Morgan's got some of the old gang working for him up there. But the two of us can take 'em, partner. We were always a good team, and I can sure account for Morgan — '

'Sorry.'

'Sorry ain't going to take, mister.'

The change in Damaron's tone halted Wilson in his tracks. And in that hanging moment the loyal *segundo* seemed to see clearly for the first time the full shocking change in his fellow survivor of the hell of Rio Toro. He'd always thought of Damaron as the swashbuckler all the women fell for. But this was no handsome gun hero sitting his broken down nag before him. With his twisted jaw, hollow, burning eyes and ravaged cheeks there was not a single 'flash' feature left about Flash Damaron. He was a man sick and old before his time, even if likely lethal still. But there was no way in hell that

Wilson would risk his life against the probably fatal odds.

There was a limit to any man's loyalty and rugged Wilson knew he had just reached his.

'I'm quittin', Flash.'

There was a sharp slapping sound as Damaron's hand hit gunbutt. 'Just hold it right there, mister. Nobody's going nowhere, and I swear I'll use this if you — '

Damaron broke off abruptly, realizing to his astonishment that Wilson — loyal, dependable, predictable Wilson — suddenly looked like a lethal and desperate stranger as his hand streaked to his gun handle and his eye glittered with murderous resentment and defiance.

Damaron recovered instantly and went for iron. He knew he'd never been quicker — that he'd executed what was surely the most desperate draw of a lifetime. But nothing could make up for those precious split-seconds' advantage in which Wilson was able to come clear and jerk trigger.

The crash of both guns came so close together they sounded as one. Mortally hit, Wilson began to slide from his saddle, his face an awful sudden white. Damaron's lopsided face attempted to deliver a smile of triumph before the lightning-bolt of agony leapt through his body and he realized that he too had been hit harder than ever before in his gunfighter's life. So hard indeed that he could not seem to breathe or feel anything, could only see the trees that danced like demons all about him before his face smashed into the hard earth and blood gushed from his mouth.

With Wilson sprawled on his face in a spreading pool of blood close by, and his own pain so intense he could no longer even feel it, he did not believe any of it could be happening to Flash Damaron . . . and then he was dead.

★　★　★

Morgan looked up sharply from his meal in the kitchen, head cocked, eyes intense.

'What?' grunted Clooney from across the table.

'Shots!' he said, dabbing at his lips with a napkin as he rose with some of his old speed and lightness to cross to the window. Then, looking out at the southern hills, his big body relaxed. 'Oh yeah,' he said, turning back to the others. 'The wolvers . . . must be them.'

'You mean those three geezers that stopped by yesterday, Morg?' Crazy Jake said around a jawful of vittles.

'Uh huh. I told 'em they could work the south valley, but not the hill. Maybe I'd better go set them straight and — '

'And let good chow get cold?' Clooney finished for him in his crochety way. 'Want my advice?'

'Reckon I'll get it if I want it or not.' Morgan half grinned.

'Sure will. Just set down and finish your supper,' the older man said. 'These are good vittles.'

Morgan glanced at his wife who nodded in agreement. He resumed his seat. Clooney was right, as usual. The vittles were first-class and he'd never tasted better.

THE END

We do hope that you have enjoyed reading this large print book.

Did you know that all of our titles are available for purchase?

We publish a wide range of high quality large print books including:
Romances, Mysteries, Classics
General Fiction
Non Fiction and Westerns

Special interest titles available in large print are:
The Little Oxford Dictionary
Music Book, Song Book
Hymn Book, Service Book

Also available from us courtesy of Oxford University Press:
Young Readers' Dictionary
(large print edition)
Young Readers' Thesaurus
(large print edition)

For further information or a free brochure, please contact us at:
Ulverscroft Large Print Books Ltd.,
The Green, Bradgate Road, Anstey,
Leicester, LE7 7FU, England.
Tel: (00 44) **0116 236 4325**
Fax: (00 44) **0116 234 0205**

A MAN CALLED SAVAGE

Sydney J. Bounds

In New York, an agent hired by the head of the Pinkerton agency would gain the respect of any law-breaker. But is Allan Pinkerton mistaken with this baby-faced killer named Savage? His task: to break up two gangs terrorizing the south-west. Armed with a shotgun — and his concealed knife — he must infiltrate and destroy both gangs, a seemingly impossible mission. Can he justify Pinkerton's faith, or will he die of lead poisoning?

SIX-GUN PRODIGAL

Ken Brompton

Lew Clennan returned to Tinkettle Basin with a price on his head, a six-gun at his hip and a grudge. His bushwhacked father and brothers lay in their graves in the basin, where the vicious code of the grass-war now held sway. Clennan rode a jump ahead of the bounty hunters to buck landgrabber Eli Brix, his gunhawks and crooked hangers-on. Soon the whole basin knew that the six-gun prodigal was back on the scene in pursuit of vengeance.

STAGE RAIDER

Luther Chance

The stage out of Harper's Town bound for Rainwater was late leaving — a bad omen for driver Charlie Deakin. The passenger list caused him further anxiety, including as it did the troublesome banker Willard Pierce and his provocative wife Madelaine; the salacious storekeeper, Lemuel Buthnott; the stranger, Holden; and gunslinger Mr Jones. Then there was the desert route, which Charlie hated, and the prospect of unwelcome riders approaching fast in a cloud of dust. Bad omens could sometimes only get darker . . .

SILVER CREEK TRAIL

David Bingley

In Silver Creek, it seemed that Dan Lawrence had been involved with two successive shooting deaths. So there was little wonder when he panicked and took off for parts unknown. His employer, Hector Morissey, had guaranteed Dan's appearance in court with $10,000, which he now stood to lose. Morissey's detective brother, Ed, went after Dan, risking his life against the bullets of Dan's outlaw associates. But Dan's final determination to do what was right made it all worthwhile.

DEAD MAN'S HAND

John Dyson

Sixty thousand dollars had been stolen from the Central Pacific, the second biggest train robbery in the US. Less than half had been recovered, and the authorities wanted to know why. Texas Ranger Clint Anderson rode south of the border, in search of the lost loot, not suspecting the trouble ahead. Pitted against corrupt *rurales*, bloodthirsty *bandidos* and backstabbers from his own brigade, whom can he trust? And as his battle reaches an explosive climax, will he lose all?